ICE VE

Against the advice of Dr Kurt Rothwell, Sarah Barford is appointed nurse on the exploration trawler,
Ice Venture. Trying to prove she is every bit as
capable as a male nurse is almost impossible while
the difficult Dr Rothwell is intent on proving his
point . . .

ICE VENTURE NURSE

BY

LYDIA BALMAIN

MILLS & BOON LIMITED
London · Sydney · Toronto

First published in Great Britain 1983
by Mills & Boon Limited, 15–16 Brook's Mews,
London W1A 1DR

Australian copyright 1983
Philippine copyright 1983

ISBN 0 263 74325 X

40,182

Set in 11 on 11½ pt Linotron Times
03/0783

Photoset by Rowland Phototypesetting Ltd
Bury St Edmunds, Suffolk
Made and printed in Great Britain by
Richard Clay (The Chaucer Press) Ltd
Bungay, Suffolk

CHAPTER ONE

'Is THAT the ship? She looks awfully small, Sarah.'

'Yes, she does look small when you think where she'll be heading,' Sarah admitted, looking at the *Ice Venture* where she lay close to the quay. 'But the whole purpose of the exercise is to see how best to help trawlers and trawlermen to stand up to Arctic conditions, so of course they had to use a genuine trawler, I suppose.'

Lucy Smith wrapped her scarlet-lined cloak more firmly around her uniform and shivered in the chill of the late January afternoon, then took her friend's arm.

'Well, it's a bit late to beg you to change your mind, so I won't try, but I hope you won't regret it. Can I come aboard with you to settle you in?'

'Darling, of course you can. If Dr Carruthers is aboard, I'll introduce you to him and you can see why I took the job with such alacrity. Though he seemed very dry, at our first meeting.'

'You're supposed to be sailing quite soon, aren't you?' Lucy said a trifle apprehensively as they gained the deck. 'I've got no desire to be carried out to sea, I can tell you, so at the first sign of movement I'm going to cut and run.'

'Supposed? We *are* sailing quite soon.' Sarah glanced around. 'Where is everyone?'

As she spoke a young man, well muffled against

the cold, emerged from the bowels of the ship and glanced across at them.

'Hello, have you lost your way? Or are you looking for someone?'

'Thank goodness, I was beginning to wonder whether this was the *Marie Celeste*,' Sarah said gaily, giving the young man her most melting smile. 'I'm Sarah Barford, or should I say Staff Nurse Barford, late of the Melton General? Anyway, I'm Dr Carruthers' assistant.'

'Oh!' The young man's voice was a trifle blank. 'You're both girls, I thought you were a fellow in that . . . sorry, it's the . . .'

Laughing, Sarah cut across his stammered explanation.

'I know, what with the parka and my cords and sea-boots, I probably look just like any other trawlerman. But I'm looking for the sick bay, and for my cabin; could you show me where it is, please?'

Lucy noticed with amusement that the young man, having recovered from his surprise, was as struck by Sarah as most men were. Indeed, with the fur of the parka framing her face and her large, dark eyes sparkling with excitement, Lucy thought that Sarah had never looked lovelier nor more feminine, despite the navy-blue cords tucked into the hefty rubber boots.

'Of course. Follow me.' He set off, then belatedly turned to them, a hand held out. 'I must be mad! My name's Stan Fitch; I'm your friendly weatherman, or shall be for the next few weeks.'

'Nice to meet you.' Sarah shook his hand vigorously. 'This is Lucy Smith, about to become Sister of a ward at the Melton General, the fortunate creature!'

'Nice to know you, Lucy.' They were below now, in a narrow corridor, and the young man—Stan—gestured to the doors flanking it. 'Galley there, mess deck next door, and then, further up, the third door along is your cabin, Sarah. May I call you Sarah?'

'Yes, of course.' Sarah pushed back her hood, revealing the richly curling, dark red hair which contrasted so well with her milky skin and dark eyes. 'And the sick bay?'

'Opposite your cabin. Though I wouldn't go in there yet, if I were you. They're unpacking stuff, and though Dr Rothwell's a brilliant man, he's inclined to be a bit short-tempered. Besides, we'll all meet at dinner—there's a bell which they ring, apparently.'

'I see. Where do we dine, then?'

Stan blinked and pulled off a woolly cap to rub a hand over rough, light-coloured hair.

'Oh, I should have shown you round, only with so much happening . . . We eat in the mess deck, to leave the officers' dining cabin free for the crew. What do you think of the accommodation?'

Sarah glanced round. There was a locker with a sizeable mirror above it and plenty of drawers for her clothes and belongings, beside a bunk, well supplied with blankets, situated just below the double-glazed porthole.

'It's nice. A bit bare, but I can soon remedy that.'

Stan laughed but shook his head.

'You mustn't do anything of the sort! Cabins have to be bare, and if you've got anything break-

able, any ornaments or bottles of scent, you'd best
let Lucy take them back to the hospital and keep
them for you, because Arctic seas are the roughest
in the world and anything standing about will be in
smithereens within ten seconds of being left. Now
look, there's something I should . . .'

'Stan? Fitch, where are you, for God's sake?'

Stan looked guilty and made for the door.

'Sorry girls, I'll have to dash, that sounds like
Kurt calling.' He left the cabin, closing the door
behind him, and they heard him clattering away
down the corridor and calling, 'Coming, sir!' in a
voice very nearly as stentorian as that which had
hailed him.

Left alone, the two girls exchanged wry glances.
Lucy spoke first.

'Sarah, are you sure you're doing the right thing?
I know it would be difficult, but you could go and
eat your words to Miss Davids and ask for your job
back. Or you could go over her head, see someone
. . .'

'No way! My boats are burned, ducky,' Sarah
said decisively, unlocking her suitcase and throwing back the lid. 'Every time I saw Davids staring at
me, I could see Geriatrics reflected in her mad, evil
eyes, and I've washed enough bottoms and soaked
enough corns this past year to last me until I've got
corns of my own to soak! Anyway, this will be an
adventure, don't you understand? Also, Dr Carruthers promised that if I did well here, he'd recommend me to a friend of his who employs nurses on
cruise ships.' She closed her eyes and smiled ecsta-
tically. 'Sunshine, blue seas, and half the Royal
Navy at my beck and call. Oh, no, She-Who-Must-

be-Obeyed can hurl bedpans at someone else for a change!'

'You wouldn't have Royal Navy officers on a cruise ship, Sarah,' Lucy, ever practical, pointed out. 'Though I suppose any sort of male would be preferable to Geriatrics, if you feel so strongly about it.' She eyed Sarah's unpacking with interest. 'You aren't going to wear that in bed, are you? Not in the Arctic.'

Sarah held up the pale blue wisp of nylon which was her best nightie and raised her brows.

'Why not? This cabin's centrally heated, and I'm not sharing it with anyone. I'll add a sweater or two if I'm chilly.' She glanced sideways at Lucy. 'Or a midshipman!'

Lucy giggled.

'The things you say! What if you're seasick, though? Suppose you spend all the time . . . What was that?'

'Heavens, it felt like a bump.' The rattle and roar of machinery interrupted her and Sarah put up the hood of her parka and hurried over to the door. 'We'd best be quick about it and get back on deck, Lucy, or you'll find yourself sailing as well as me. That's the engines warming up.'

'Oh, mercy!' Lucy trotted anxiously in her friend's wake, wrapping her cloak about her once more. 'And I didn't take your breakables either, Sarah.'

'I haven't got any, or hardly any,' Sarah said cheerfully. 'Give my love to the girls and tell them I'll come and see them as soon as we dock.'

As the two girls hurried along the companionway a man came towards them. He was very tall, very dark, and very annoyed about something, judging from the expression on his face. As he drew level with them he flattened himself against the bulkhead, for there was not room for them all to pass in the narrow corridor. His dark eyes took them in at a glance, and did not appear to approve of what they saw.

'Hurry up, ladies, all ashore,' he said crisply. 'All visitors, that is. We're sailing because the tide's right and everyone's checked in at last.'

'I'm sorry, I'm just going, we didn't know . . .' Lucy began, smiling nervously up at the tall man.

'Well, you know now.' He pushed past them and continued on his way. Sarah turned and stared after him, scowling.

'What a rude pig! I hope I don't have much to do with him, unless it's as a patient, when I'd teach him a few manners if it was the last thing I did. Mind you, he's probably crew, he looked like a seaman, didn't he?'

'He was gorgeous, whoever he is,' Lucy said frankly as they gained the deck. 'If I'd known the crew were going to be like that, I'd have asked for an interview for the job as well.'

'That's the type of male chauvinist who wants you to lie down and let him plant his wretched trotters all over you, and then expects you to be grateful,' Sarah said reproachfully, then threw her arms round her friend and kissed her cheek. 'Cheerio darling, and a thousand thanks for seeing me off. I'll come straight up to Cas. the moment we dock—you'll still be in Casualty in six to eight weeks, I suppose?'

Lucy ran down the gangplank and turned to face her friend.

'Cheek! I intend to be the best Casualty Sister the General's ever known. Take care, love.'

The ship was not moving, but she was throbbing, and Lucy was disappearing into the early dusk so Sarah turned back towards her cabin. Rather indecisively, she made her way along the corridor, then paused outside the sick bay. She had only met Dr Carruthers once, at the interview for the job of nurse aboard the *Ice Venture*, and though she had told Lucy all about him, she was privately none too sure that she would recognise him again. He was past middle-age, greying, authoritative, but more than that she could not say, and she had no desire to go into the sick bay and accost the wrong man. No, it might be better to stay in her cabin until someone came and fetched her.

She entered the small room, closed the door behind her, and sat on the edge of the bunk. That Stan Fitch had been rather nice; he had said he was a weatherman, which meant that she now knew, more or less, two members of the team of scientists who would spend the voyage trying out ice-fighting techniques, forecasting weather conditions, studying whatever flora and fauna there was in the cold Northern seas, and, in the case of Dr Carruthers, taking care of the team themselves and those of the crew who were aboard.

Her own particular part in this scheme was to nurse anyone who might fall ill or be hurt, of course, and to carry out various tests on those who remained hale and hearty. Dr Carruthers had showed her sample tests which she would be perfectly capable of carrying out without any sort of supervision, and others which she would need help with, at first at any rate. Blood pressure, pulse rate, temperatures, would be checked as a matter of course two or three times a day, and Dr Carruthers himself would give her lists of questions which everyone would be required to fill in, whenever they had the leisure.

She wondered what the other members of the team would be like. Dr Carruthers, in his late fifties, would be the oldest, she imagined. There were to be six team members including herself and seven crew including the captain. Also, there would be a cook.

She was still sitting on her bunk when the ship lurched into motion, making her glance at her wristwatch. Gracious, it was getting quite late, and she was still in her outdoor things. She wondered whether she ought to slip her uniform on, for she had been provided with some hospital dresses and aprons by the thoughtful doctor as soon as he told her she had the job. But on reflection, she decided against this. Dinner, after all, was a semi-social occasion, and she did have rather a special dress. She had unpacked all her clothing and, with some regret, had put it neatly into the locker provided, for there was no wardrobe space where she might have hung clothes up. Now she went to the top drawer of the locker and shook out the rather special dress. Smoke-blue, made of very fine Indian cotton, with a low neckline and very full sleeves tightly cuffed to the wrist, she knew it suited her, knew it looked good with her navy suede court shoes and with her hair tied up on top like a

Japanese lady's and held there with a smoke-blue velvet band.

She had shed her shaggy black sweater and the navy cords and was standing before the mirror in her bra and briefs, spraying perfume at her cleavage, when there was a perfunctory tap on the door and it burst open. The tall man she and Lucy had met earlier entered the cabin.

'Barford, we're all . . .' He stopped short. Sarah grabbed for her dress and held it defensively against herself and saw his mouth tighten. 'What's this? Who the hell are you and what the devil are you doing in this cabin?'

Sarah, arranging the dress around herself, sarifashion, gulped and began to reply, but he was across the room in a couple of strides and grabbing her shoulders.

'This is intolerable! Do you know this is a scientific expedition to the very edge of the Polar cap, to find out . . .'

Sarah, regaining her self-possession now that she was more or less respectable again, also regained the use of her tongue. Flushing hotly, she wrenched herself out of his grip and shouted back at him, every bit as loudly as he had just shouted at her,

'How dare you burst into my cabin without warning? And why are you yelling at me? Where's Dr Carruthers? This is my cabin, and when he hears what I've got to say . . .'

The man made no attempt to touch her again, but his black brows lowered themselves into a scowl and his expression changed from fury to icy contempt.

'Oh no, not another of Dr Carruthers' little

jokes! For the last time, who are you and what are you doing here?'

'I'm Sarah Barford, a state registered nurse and Dr Carruthers' assistant.'

He continued to look down at her, his expression not at all friendly.

'Why, that doddering old fool, how dare he try to saddle the expedition with a woman!' For the first time, his eyes strayed from her face to her person and he saw her desperate clutching at the folds of her dress. His firm mouth quirked and his expression softened a little. 'Look, I'm sorry I bawled you out, I daresay you had no idea that Dr Carruthers was exceeding his duty by appointing you. Get your dress on and I'll make some radio calls and arrange for you to be taken off.'

He turned back towards the door, but Sarah's temper was now thoroughly up. Dress or no dress, she crossed the room and grabbed at the sleeve of his dark sweater.

'Oh no you don't! "Exceeding his duty", what do you mean? I was appointed to be Dr Carruthers' assistant, it's nothing whatever to do with you! Who are you, anyway?'

He turned back. Signs of softening had disappeared, to be replaced by annoyance, Sarah noticed.

'I'm Dr Kurt Rothwell, the leader of this expedition.'

'The leader? But Dr Carruthers . . .'

'Gave you the impression he was leading the expedition, did he? All he was doing, young lady, absolutely all, was some rather unimportant spade work in the research field. He volunteered to help out by setting some questionnaires, getting some of the necessary equipment together, and finding us a nurse who could act as my assistant. A *male* nurse, of course.'

Sarah's finely-arched brows rose.

'Did you specify a male nurse?'

'Of course. Or, if not in so many words, I certainly gave him the information that it was to be an all-male team. Damn it, the man knew very well what I wanted!'

'Yet he did appoint me,' Sarah began stubbornly. 'And I fail to see . . .'

'Fortunately, whether you see or not is immaterial. You'll be taken ashore as soon as I can arrange it. We'll manage without a nursing assistant.'

Before she could utter more than an outraged gasp he had walked out of the cabin, slamming the door closed behind him.

Simmering, Sarah dragged her dress on, pushed her feet into her shoes and marched after him, flashing a glance in the mirror as she passed it on her way to the door.

It stopped her in her tracks. Her face was devoid of makeup, her hair half up and half down, she wore no tights and even her dress, dragged on as it had been, was not looking its best. With a sigh, she turned back. At the end of five minutes the Sarah Barford who looked back at her from the mirror was as poised and well-groomed as she could wish. She picked up her clutch handbag, tossed her head, and made for the sick bay.

She opened the door without knocking and gazed challengingly at the man who sat behind the desk, facing her across the room.

'Dr Rothwell, may I remind you that though Dr Carruthers may have been wrong to appoint me, his was not the signature on my letter of appointment. Nor was it worded in such a way that I might assume Dr Carruthers to be my employer. In other words, a committee or a group of people are backing this expedition and, strictly speaking, it is they who employed me.'

'That's true, because everyone, myself included, assumed that S. Barford was a male nurse. No one dreamed that Carruthers would be fool enough to employ a girl to nurse a dozen men aboard a trawler in the Arctic! So that cuts no ice, Nurse!'

Sarah closed her eyes and shuddered delicately.

'I abhor puns, Dr Rothwell.'

She opened her eyes and looked across at him. He was grinning.

'It was unintentional, as it happens. I'm sorry for your disappointment and I'm sure we'll pay any expenses you may have incurred because of the mistake, but it just isn't on. I'm composing a radio message now, and we'll get a boat to come out and take you off, so all's well that end's well.'

'Look, you expected a nurse and you've got one. My nursing experience obviously satisfied you, and . . .'

'It's no use, Miss Barford, I'm sending you back. We've got enough doctors aboard, heaven knows.'

'But only one is medically qualified, and that's you,' Sarah pointed out crisply. 'If there are accidents or illnesses, if you have to operate, then you'll need a nurse, you know you will. And though no doubt someone else can take temperatures and b.p's, check pulse rates, write up your notes, haven't the team enough to do without adding clerical work to the rest? Dr Carruthers was most insistent that whoever got the job could type quickly and accurately, and take shorthand notes, too. Or are you adept at such things, and also capable of being in two places at once?'

He could not have failed to notice the vinegar behind that last bit, but his face remained calm and determined.

'It's true that it won't be easy, but it's better, to be frank, than having a woman aboard. This isn't my first trip into the Arctic and I don't mind admitting it's no picnic, so I'm afraid not your prettiest wiles will persuade me. I'm sending you home, Miss Barford.'

'If you do, I'll go straight to the nearest equal opportunities board, or whatever it's called, and sue you!'

He was out of his chair and round the desk so fast that she could not have escaped even if she had wanted to do so. He caught hold of her and shook her, his fingers digging into her arm so hard that she winced.

'Do you want to be the only woman on a small vessel with a dozen or so men, for six weeks, possibly longer? We'll face danger, great discomfort, perhaps even death. If I let you stay and you got into any sort of trouble, the blame would be mine. To be blunt, you could be killed or injured whatever your sex, but only a woman runs the risk of rape.'

'Rape?' Sarah's eyes widened incredulously. 'Don't be absurd! The men aboard are scientists, not animals, and the crew have been hand-picked for their efficiency and knowledge of the conditions, Dr Carruthers told me so.'

He shrugged. He had blue eyes, she noticed, but now they were ice-hard and watched her closely.

'You're a very pretty girl, you can't be more than twenty. None of the men aboard expect to have to cope with the emotional business of having an unattached woman with us. Extreme danger brings out the best and the worst in people. And look at you!' He flicked her low neckline with a contemptuous finger. 'I can't spend all my time seeing that you don't get into some sort of trouble!'

'You wouldn't have to. I can take care of myself.'

'It isn't just that. Suppose you take a fancy to one of the men, just flirting, encouraging them to flirt with you. There may be no harm in it from your point of view, but it can lead to rivalry, bad feeling, all the things I least want to see on board this ship.'

Sarah felt her face flame. What did he think she was, some sort of nymphomaniac? As if she would flirt.

'I've been around long enough not to do anything so foolish, and anyway, I'm twenty-three, and I've nursed on a male surgical ward for two years before I got put onto Geriatrics. No one ever complained about my behaviour towards the patients, nor theirs towards me.'

He sighed in an exaggerated manner.

'Sick men rarely pounce; these men aren't sick, Nurse! Look at it from another angle; we've got one shower room divided into six cubicles, one lavatory, divided into three cubicles. Can't you *see*? This whole ship is geared for one sex, not two.'

'I'll manage.' She kept her gaze steady. 'You

won't regret letting me stay, I promise you.'

'And then there's the work,' he went on re-morselessly. 'The crew will do all the actual sailing, but keeping the ice down, cleaning the ship, bringing in coal for the galley fire, emptying slops, things like that, will all be work for the team. You couldn't handle an axe or direct a steam hose. You might be willing, but you aren't physically strong enough for most of those jobs.'

'I can fetch coal and empty slops,' Sarah said obstinately. 'And I can nurse the sick, do first-aid on minor injuries, and keep your notes up to date.'

'And cope with an amorous man in a force eight gale?'

Sarah sighed.

'If you must know, I'm inoculated against men at the moment. Until three months ago I was engaged to a successful young barrister, we were planning a June wedding next year, everything seemed set for success.'

'And?'

'And I found that during his twice-weekly visits to London, to study court procedure, he was living with another girl.'

His cynical expression grew more pronounced.

'Inoculated against men by one unfortunate experience? I wonder!'

Before she could move, he had caught her in his arms. There was a brief, undignified struggle, Sarah began to splutter out a protest, and then his mouth claimed hers. She was crushed against him, feeling her breasts pressing against the rough wool of her jersey whilst his hands moved down her back, sliding over her hips, arching her against him. And all the while his mouth worked at hers until her lips parted and then, for a moment, she forgot who he was, where they were, and knew only the pleasure that his mouth was bringing, the warmth of his hands, the warm smell of him in her nostrils.

He pushed her back from him and she opened her eyes, horrified to realise that they had closed, and looked up into his face. He smiled down at her sarcastically, one brow climbing.

'Inoculated? I think not!'

Hot with humiliation, Sarah felt tears rise to her eyes and fought to hold them back. She could not let him see how silly she felt, so she held his gaze, then spoke with admirable steadiness.

'That, Dr Rothwell, was merely a physical reaction caused by shock. You used your superior strength against me when I wasn't expecting it. Now that I know the depths to which you can sink, I can promise you it won't happen again.'

He smiled. It was not a pleasant smile.

'It had better not happen again, Nurse. Very well, if you're sure you can cope, then I'll take you along to the mess deck and introduce you to the rest of the team.' His eyes dropped to her mouth and lingered there. 'But before we go, perhaps you'd better . . . tidy yourself up a little.'

She turned on her heel and swept back into her cabin, closing the door behind her with a snap. Looking in the mirror, she saw that her mouth was smudged from his kiss and her cheeks still far too pink. She compressed her lips. Hateful, conceited man, to assume that an automatic—and slight—response to a kiss had been anything other than the normal behaviour of anyone caught off balance, as

she had been. She tidied her hair, applied a wet
flannel to her mouth and then reapplied her lip-
stick. Only when she felt perfectly self-assured
once more did she go back to the corridor, where he
awaited her.

'Ready, Nurse Barford?'

He was smiling down at her almost encouraging-
ly. Having made up his mind to let her stay, it
seemed as though he were going to be generous.
She smiled back at him, with a gaiety which she
hoped would belie the doubts which he had seeded
in her mind.

'Ready, Dr Rothwell!'

CHAPTER TWO

THE rest of the team were a pleasant crowd and they hid their surprise over finding a woman aboard very well, assuring Sarah that she was welcome.

Stan, the weather expert who had been first to greet her on her arrival aboard, introduced her to Albert Leman, Fred Bolton and Alan Wilde, who were investigating the possibility of various sea-weeds and plankton as food, and to David Butcher, Don Whitfield and Phil Riley, all of whom were engaged in investigating the improvement of ice-fighting and fishing techniques. All the men were under forty, all of them physically fit, and Sarah soon realised that they had one other thing in common—a great respect for Dr Rothwell.

'Kurt's gone along as medical adviser on three or four polar expeditions, so he doesn't just know it in theory, he's actually experienced the conditions we're trying to improve, which is more than the rest of us have,' Don explained, when he, Sarah and the cook, Hughie, were working in the galley five days after their departure from the port. 'You may sniff, my girl, but he's a man I'm proud to work for.'

'I'm sure he's admirable in many ways,' Sarah said, vigorously rolling out scone mixture on the well-scrubbed galley table. 'But he's so dictatorial, Don! Besides, he's still furious with me because I'm a woman.'

Don, peeling potatoes at the sink, turned to grin at her.

'I'm very glad you're a woman! "Oh, good, a cuddly woman to comfort us amidst the winter snow," I thought, when I first clapped eyes on you.'

Sarah laughed.

'Very funny! But Kurt really thinks I'm a fatal mistake—or should I say a *femme fatale* mistake?' She ducked as Don threw a sliver of potato peel at her. 'He's threatened to keelhaul me if I so much as cause one of you lot to glance away from a scientific experiment for a moment, so just you get on with those potatoes and ignore me.'

'I wouldn't call peeling spuds scientific experimentation, exactly,' Don grumbled mildly, turning back to the sink. 'How many more do you want done, Hughie? I seem to have peeled the entire output of Pembrokeshire already.'

'There's enough there,' Hughie said, peering into the sink. 'A good spud basher you are, Don.'

'I'm famous for it,' Don boasted, turning gleefully from the sink. 'Lord, the state my hands will be in!' He winked at Sarah. 'I'm going up on deck to get some temperature readings. Coming?'

'Mm hmm. When I've put this last batch of scones into the oven.' Sarah began placing the rounds on a greased tray. 'Don't wait for me, Don, I'll follow you up.'

The cold outside was intense already, and both crew and team members were used to being well wrapped up before going on deck so Sarah knew that it would take Don a few moments to get into his parka, muffler, mittens and boots. For her part, she was wearing her boots already, since they had better gripping soles and heels than any other footwear she possessed, and her parka was hanging on the hook behind the kitchen door, all ready for use. She enjoyed trips onto the deck, despite the cold, and went out whenever she could to escape from the fug which frequently built up below.

She was working very hard at present to try to make Dr Rothwell see she was both efficient and sensible, with what success, however, she could not have told. He made it plain that he had high standards and expected her to keep up to them, and watched her efforts impassively, though he was quick enough, she thought bitterly, to pick her up on anything which was not done as he wanted it done. However, he had not found many causes for complaint yet, to her relief.

Now, putting the last batch of scones into the oven, she turned thankfully to Hughie.

'There we are, all done! If you could just get them out, Hughie, in about fifteen to twenty minutes, I can join Don on deck. It's a nice, clear afternoon and everyone keeps telling me that it'll be night all day long soon, so I want to take a look round while I can.'

'Off with you then, gal,' Hughie said genially. He was a hugely fat man with rolling chins, little, bright eyes almost hidden behind bulging cheeks, and an incongruous crew-cut on his gingery hair. Despite his size, however, he managed to squeeze his way around the tiny galley, cooking and serving the most delicious meals. 'Thanks for your help.'

'A pleasure. See you!'

Sarah, well muffled, climbed the companionway, unlatched the door at the top, and clambered out onto the deck, shutting the door behind her. It would not do to leave it open, for the sea was rough and waves frequently swamped the deck.

Sarah glanced round for Don, then spotted him on the brightly-lit bridge with Dr Rothwell. He seemed absorbed in something, but would doubtless come out soon. Although she had said it was clear, in fact it was duskish already, and the arc-lights which would illumine the deck once the ship was in the region of eternal night would only be lit when there were men working on deck, so she strolled over to the rail and looked around her. A faint hump on the horizon might have been land, or, again, it might have been cloud. But the air was fresh and clean even when breathed through a muffler, and she stayed where she was, enjoying the invigorating, salt-laden breeze.

She glanced towards the bridge, and saw Dr Rothwell was watching her. Quickly, she looked out to sea again, with an impatient sigh. So she was not to be free of the eagle eye even here, it seemed! Well, he could scarcely criticise her behaviour alone on deck, with only the sound of the ship's engines and the cry of a solitary gull for company.

It was then that she noticed the gull properly for the first time. It was a magnificent bird, but it seemed to be in some sort of trouble, for it glided round the deck and then came in to land on the rigging. But something was wrong, for instead of gripping with its feet it made a sort of inefficient jab at the line which stretched between the funnel and the whaleback, then fell heavily onto the deck.

'Hello, what's wrong?' Sarah approached the bird cautiously. It drew back its head and hissed like a goose, then began to flap frenziedly, trying to get away from her. Firmly, Sarah seized the bird round the body, though not without a good deal of resistance. 'Come on, old fellow, I only want to help!'

The gull, however, seemed reluctant to believe her. It gave an indignant squawk and beat with its huge wings, and for a moment actually rose in the air so that Sarah had a nightmare vision of herself being carried off, dangling from its streamlined grey body, to some distant, icy peak.

However, all that actually happened was that a strong wing hit her across the face, a taloned foot raked across a section of wrist where sleeve and mitten had parted, and Sarah swore and tried to throw the bird upwards so that it could fly away, but her captive only lurched sideways onto the deck again.

Baffled, Sarah bent again, and this time succeeded in getting a firm grip on the bird's body. Now she could see what the trouble was. Oil, thick and dark, smothered one of the bird's mighty wings and a part of its tail, so that when it was airborne it was lopsided, forced to fly almost in half-circle by the encumbered, useless feathers.

'I'll take you down to the sickbay and clean you up,' Sarah muttered. A wing, oil-laden, flapped across her mouth and Sarah and gull gave a simultaneous scream of exasperation. 'Stay *still*, you damned fool!'

'Let me!'

Two strong, lean hands, unencumbered by mittens, reached over her shoulder and trapped the bird's wings to its sides. The gull, reduced abruptly from a creature of heraldry to ducklike submission, sat and blinked in Dr Rothwell's hold. Sarah, brushing an oily mitten across one flushed cheek, let out her breath in a long whistle of relief.

'Whew! Thanks very much. I'm afraid he's a bit too much for me.'

Dr Rothwell looked down at her, a grin lurking.

'A bit too much? I thought at one point that he was going to take off and carry you with him! Didn't it occur to you to trap his wings so that he couldn't keep beating you about the head with them?' His gaze travelled over her face. 'I daresay you don't know you're as black as the ace of spades?'

'Oh damn, am I?' They reached the companion-way and she preceded him down it. 'He's awfully strong, you know.'

'He has to be, to live in this climate. Open the door for me, would you?'

Fumbling with the sickbay door handle beneath his impatient gaze, Sarah had to remove her mitten to open it cleanly. As she did so, she caught a cold glance from the gull's eyes which reminded her of someone. But who?

'Come along, Nurse, you rescued this creature so you can clean him up! Get some liquid paraffin down for a start, and some cottonwool.'

Sarah shed her outer clothing and reached the required articles down from their respective shelves, then spread a disposable sheet across their small operating table.

'Very well, Doctor. Only I don't think he'll like it!'

'He'll be all right, provided he's handled firmly.' He grinned across at her, a lock of his dark hair flopping rather attractively across his brow. 'Birds are like women, handle them firmly and with authority and they come to heel very nicely; let them start flapping and you'll never control them.'

'There speaks the voice of experience,' Sarah said drily, pouring liquid paraffin onto a large pad of cottonwool. 'Shall I start with his feet?'

'Go ahead.'

Twenty minutes later, considerably battered but with a clean and oil-free gull in a cardboard box at their feet, doctor and nurse stared at each other across the wreck of the disposable sheet.

'Handled firmly, he behaved just like a woman, didn't he, sir?' Sarah murmured wickedly. 'He's quite a character!'

'I refuse to rise to the bait, Nurse,' Dr Rothwell said ruefully, rubbing his tattered surgical gloves. 'Look, perch on the edge of the table and I'll sort you out next.'

'My wounds, you mean?' Sarah did as he said, ruefully examining her scratched hands. 'I've never known a patient so reluctant to be cleaned up, and I've bathed some fearful old tramps in my time.'

'I'm sure you have. Push back your hair, I'll start with your face.'

The stuff stung, but Sarah suffered in silence, knowing that she must get rid of the oil. Once he said 'Close your eyes,' and she did so and felt the pad of soaked cottonwool passing firmly over lids and lashes. Then he said, 'Open them again now,' and she did so, to find his face near her own, his eyes squinting slightly as he concentrated on rubbing a smear of oil off her nose.

'That's better. Now for some soap and water.'

'I can do that,' Sarah protested, trying to get up, but he pushed her down again.

'I finish a job once I start. There!'

The towel patted her dry and she opened her eyes again to find his face, this time, only inches from her own. His eyes were on her mouth and he was smiling. She wanted, suddenly, to jump down from the table, to busy herself over something. But she could not do so without pushing him away.

'Nice and clean, like a little girl ready for bed.' Before she could move his mouth brushed hers, then returned more firmly. Then he moved away and his hands gripped her waist. 'Down with you! Now you can clean me up, and throw away the disposable sheet, and my rubber gloves, which will never be the same again.'

Just as though nothing had happened, Sarah thought, throwing the shattered sheet into the waste-bin and peeling off his gloves. He sat, as she had done, on the edge of the operating table, then stood up and glanced round.

'No good, you'd never reach me to get the gunge off my face—or did I manage to avoid that? My wrists seem to have borne the brunt of it.'

'Your face is clean, sir,' Sarah said with inward thankfulness. 'You can sit on the table for me to do your hands and wrists.'

Presently, both cleaned up, they looked down at their patient.

'Well, Nurse? What do you recommend?'

'Bed rest?' suggested Sarah.

'Probably, though not in any bed of mine! Take him down to the galley, I daresay Hughie knows a bit about exhausted gulls.'

Sarah felt she could scarcely take the bird down there in an open cardboard box just when Hughie was at his busiest preparing the evening meal, so she took the bird along to her cabin, put the box down by her bunk, and went to the galley, secretly thinking that the cook would laugh at her, but this did not prove to be the case. Hughie told her that trawlermen often rescued exhausted birds and that he had a coop built for the purpose of housing the travellers until they were well enough to leave once more.

'Bring 'im down to the galley, gal,' he said kindly. 'Partial to a bit of stale bread soaked in rum, gulls is. I'll get some.'

'He's in a smallish cardboard box at the moment, he'll much prefer that coop,' Sarah said. 'I'll fetch him.'

This proved easier said than done. To her dismay, when she opened her cabin door and switched on the light, the bird appeared to have flown, or walked, at any rate. The cardboard box, looking as if it had been run over by a bus, lay on its side on the floor, and at first glance she could not see the bird anywhere.

A slight hiss drew her attention to the locker. The gull was sitting with its back to the mirror, wings half raised, bill agape. He looked considerably larger than he had done when grasped by Dr Rothwell's ruthless hands on the operating table.

'You blighter,' Sarah said wearily. 'Get back into the box like a good gull, and Sarah will carry you down to the galley for some lovely rum!'

The gull stretched out its neck and made a derisive sound. Sarah sighed.

'Very well, be like that. I'll get help.'

In the end, it took half the team to re-box the gull and a good deal of noise was made in the process. The men were in full flight round the cabin, Don and Alan shouting and pursuing while Stan tried to trap the bird with the box and Sarah guarded the door, when two hands took Sarah's shoulders in an unkindly grip.

'What on earth's going on here, Nurse? Entertaining men in your cabin is strictly against the rules.'

Sarah wriggled.

'It's not my fault, Doctor, the wretched gull escaped. Oh, oh, hold him, Don, hold him!'

Don, with the gull at last in the cardboard box, bowed to right and left, spun round, and saw Dr Rothwell's grim face.

'Oh! Sorry, Kurt, we were just . . .'

'I can see. I do *not* approve of horseplay! Out of here, all of you.'

Obediently the men left the room, each going his own way while Don took the captive to the galley. Sarah and the doctor were left facing each other across the now extremely untidy cabin. Sarah lifted her chin defiantly.

'Go on, say it! Why did I appeal to them, why didn't I catch him alone? I would have, only he's quite scary, and so big . . . I admit I was scared of him.'

There was a slight softening in the blue eyes which held her own.

'Very well, I accept your explanation. But don't let it occur again, Nurse.'

Later, in the galley, gloomily feeding the gull

with bread soaked in spirit, Sarah told Hughie about the scene in her cabin.

'You'd have thought I was hostessing an orgy, honestly! The fellows were enjoying the chase, they'd have enjoyed chasing that confounded bird round anyone's cabin. Yet he made me feel guilty as hell.'

'Never mind, gal, but there's something in what he says. Discipline's important on a ship as small as this. You can't 'ave too much messing about and that's a fact. Another time, just get me, or Stan, to help, not three or four of us.'

Sarah snorted and fed the gull the last of the bread.

'Honestly, Hughie, you're so *naive*! If there'd been only one man in the cabin with Gussy gull and me I daren't *think* what wrathful Rothwell would have said!'

Hughie chuckled but shook his head.

'You're a caution, you are! He's a good fellow, the doc, you've just got to remember who's the boss.'

'I do. All the time. He never lets me forget it. Oh, I'll learn!'

Next day, having been told firmly by Dr Rothwell that he was not to be disturbed since he was working on some figures, Sarah had her first ever casualty to deal with, without a doctor's comforting presence. An engineer named Evans caught his fingers in the steel door of the engine room and his roar of agony and his subsequent appearance in the sickbay, supported by two colleagues and bleeding like a pig, struck momentary horror into Sarah's heart.

Fortunately, when she examined the fingers she found them badly torn but by no means beyond her capabilities to mend. She cleaned the wounds, then took down the equipment she would need to cope with them.

Sutures would mean calling Dr Rothwell, but in this instance, she really thought that Steristrip would be sufficient, for the engineer's fingers were thin, the wounds so placed that stitching, in any event, would have been difficult and would have meant that stiffness in the top knuckle might have resulted.

'This won't hurt,' she said reassuringly and Evans, a lad of no more than twenty, grinned palely.

'You gotta be tough to work on trawlers, Miss,' he said. 'If I scream, you slap me wrist!'

'It's a bargain.' Sarah, having cleaned the worst damaged finger, painted iodine on either side of the gash, telling the boy reassuringly that the iodine was helpful because it thoroughly dried the skin and helped the dressing to stick. Then she picked up a card of strips, peeled the back off the first, and stuck it firmly across the wound so that it held the edges close.

'I'll do this three or four times,' she told Evans, suiting action to her words. 'And then one right down the middle, to help the others to stick. Then I'll cover it with a gauze pad, like this, and you mustn't move it or get it wet. In ten days' time I'll remove the whole dressing and your fingers will be as good as new.'

'Magic!' Evans enthused, as she finished off the second wound. 'No needles, then?'

'We-ell, I think perhaps you ought to have a tiny anti-tetanus jab. But honestly, you'll hardly feel a thing.'

He grinned sceptically, but bore up well and, as she tossed the disposable syringe into the waste basket, stood up and grinned down at her, one eyebrow rising.

'Back to work, eh?'

'Light duties only.' She reached for a triangular bandage and made it into a sling, resting the injured fingers lightly in it. 'There, keep it like that until it begins to heal.'

'Pretty *and* efficient!' He grinned down at her with open admiration. 'How about coming out for a drink, when we dock?'

She smiled back.

'That's what I call thinking ahead! I might, at that. Take care of that hand, and I'll see you in ten days.'

'Right, Miss.'

Soon after Evans had left, Dr Rothwell brought in a bundle of ill-written scribble for her to type out. Taking the pages, Sarah reflected it was just her luck to have to work for a doctor who wrote his notes in the self-same unreadable scrawl which he used for prescriptions, and she was no pharmacist! However, she managed to interpret it quite well, once she took into account the fact that his vowels were almost identical at first—and sometimes second—glance.

When she had finished she took the neatly typed sheets through to the doctor's cabin, where he was working on a mass of figures which she sincerely trusted she would not be asked to type. He glanced at the work she had done, nodded, then turned towards the porthole.

'Release that gull now, and you'd better get a move on, before the light goes. What was that noise I heard just now?'

'One of the men caught his hand in a steel door. I've attended to it.'

'Good.' He nodded, brief and businesslike. 'Now send the gull off, please.'

'Already? But he's only had a day to recover, and . . .'

Her pleas for clemency were cut short.

'Don't argue, Nurse, I do know what I'm doing, though you obviously don't believe it. Take the bird up on deck and release it.'

Muttering beneath her breath, Sarah made for the galley.

'Hughie? Wake up, I've come for the gull. The boss-man says I'm to release him now.'

Hughie, asleep in his chair, stirred and then peered blearily towards the porthole.

'Said that, did 'e? Reckon he's right. If you wait till tomorrow it's likely we'll be too far north.'

'I don't see it; why should a gull mind how far north we are?' She bent and opened the coop, within which the gull dozed, yellow eyes closed. 'Come on then, my hearty, the witch doctor says you've got to be chucked out into the cold!'

But when she reached the deck there was a wicked wind howling, with flakes of snow on its breath. She stood the gull down and it remained just where it was. Exasperated, Sarah gave it a nudge and then, when that failed to work, administered what she told herself was a tiny kick. This appeared to make her message plain. The bird muttered, half opened its beak to hiss at her, and took off, flying into the gathering gloom. Sarah watched it out of sight and then returned to the warmth of the galley, where Hughie was slicing beef for a stew.

'He's gone, Hughie, and he wasn't at all keen to leave us. Were you serious when you said he had to be released now?'

Hughie nodded.

'Aye. You'll see fewer and fewer birds as we get further north. It's too cold for 'em. That gull of yours should make it now, but give him another day or so in a warm atmosphere, with us travelling north all the time, and he wouldn't stand a chance. He'd find the blood freezing in his veins, very like. At any rate, he'd not get a foot from the deck without cashing in his chips.'

'Oh!' Sarah said rather blankly. 'Then perhaps the doc does know what he's talking about.'

Hughie chuckled and began to dice vegetables for his stew.

'That's right, gal!'

'Good morning, Nurse! In working clothes, I see.'

Sarah, finishing off her breakfast on the mess deck, smiled up at Dr Rothwell, looming over her.

'That's right, sir. It's our day on in the sickbay for blood samples, so I thought I'd dress the part. Give my customers confidence, you might say.'

Dr Rothwell, who seemed to think that donning his white coat and slinging a stethoscope round his neck was a sign that he was on duty, glanced approvingly at Sarah's blue uniform dress with the crisp white apron over it and the dark blue, silver-buckled belt around it.

'You look very efficient; let's hope you manage to make everyone relax.' He flashed a menacing smile around the other breakfasters. 'For some reason the mere mention of the word "blood" seems to make strong men turn pale and not so strong ones faint. The crew are in on this blood-sampling too, and I want an example of stoicism from each and every one of my team, please.'

Don, sitting next to Sarah and crunching toast and marmalade, laughed and got up.

'It's instilled into us as kids, Kurt—we hate needles in any shape or form.' He patted Sarah's head. 'Women, having less imagination than men, don't seem to regard losing valuable amounts of blood and having needles stuck in them with much fear, though. I take it you are sampling young Sarah's gore as well as ours?'

'Naturally. And my own.' Dr Rothwell strolled towards the door. 'Come along, Nurse, I want your blood first.'

'He's frequently after my blood in one form or another,' Sarah sighed as the door closed. 'Believe it or not, Don, I have every bit as many reservations over blood samples as the average man!' She got up and went towards the door. 'But if I show any yellow streaks, Dr Rothwell will put a black mark in the ledger he's keeping on my behaviour. See you presently.'

She went along to the sickbay, and found Dr Rothwell ready for her, with a syringe in one hand, a pad of ether-soaked cottonwool in the other, and a Dracula-like smile on his countenance.

'Ah, Nurse! Sit down here, please.'

Sarah, outwardly calm, sat down and offered her arm to the dreaded needle which, very much to her relief, was being handled by Dr Rothwell with a casual confidence which did much to lighten her apprehension. Sarah belonged to the school of thought which believed that doctors, unless they specialise in taking blood samples, are rarely good at it.

'Clench your fist, Nurse. Why are you closing your eyes?'

The tourniquet band was tightened round her upper arm and Sarah rather sheepishly opened her eyes as she felt the needle slide into her vein. She saw the syringe darken and fill and knew that Dr Rothwell was as efficient as he expected others to be.

'Did I close my eyes? Sorry, sir. All done?'

The needle was removed so smoothly that she was scarcely aware of it and strong fingers pressed a pad of soaked cottonwool against the tiny mark the needle had left.

'Finished. Now you can get your revenge.'

She stood up and he promptly seated himself in her chair, rolled up his sleeve and glanced impatiently up at her.

'The syringe is ready, Nurse. Let's see how good you are at this.'

In fact, Sarah's experience of taking blood was nil, but she did not intend to let Dr Rothwell know that! She rubbed his arm in the crook of his elbow briskly with ether-soaked cottonwool and tightened the tourniquet band, then inserted the needle gingerly into the swelling vein. With hands which shook only the tiniest bit, she began to draw off the blood, and seconds later was squirting the result into the already labelled sample bottle and turning, with some relief, towards the door.

'Shall I start the men coming in now, sir?'

He looked across at her, rolling his sleeve down, and actually smiled approvingly.

'Yes, you might as well. You did that very neatly, Nurse, and you struck oil, so to speak, at the first attempt, which is a sure sign of confidence. Well done!'

'Thank you. But what made you say at the first attempt?' Sarah was on her guard. 'You make it sound as if I've never taken a blood sample before.'

Dark eyebrows climbed and Dr Rothwell's mouth curved in a sardonic smile.

'My dear girl, I don't think you ever have!'

Sarah felt her cheeks go pink.

'As a matter of fact . . .' she began, but was interrupted.

'Confession may be good for the soul, Nurse, but we've patients out there who'll be all the better for not hearing that they're to be guinea-pigs. Let them in, please!'

For two days the ship ploughed on, into the endless dark. It was very cold now, so cold that Sarah was warned never to go on deck alone, nor to remove so much as the tip of her nose from her muffler, far less incautiously take a breath of the iced air.

'If you breathe in quickly to shout or call, ice particles can form in your lungs and puncture them,' Dr Rothwell told her severely. 'Never unwind your muffler from around your face, Nurse, never take off your mittens for a moment, never linger up there longer than necessary. And, above all, never go on deck alone. The hazards are too numerous to mention.'

'Are they more numerous than the hazards encountered if I go on deck with one of the men?' Sarah asked with assumed innocence. 'I remember something about coping with an amorous man in a force eight gale . . .'

'Don't be flippant!' Dr Rothwell snapped out the words so sharply that Sarah blinked. 'Just do as you're told for once.'

That rankled. It seemed to Sarah that she spent all of her waking hours doing as she was told! But she seethed in silence, for, as the team were so quick to remind her, Kurt Rothwell was the boss.

Now, making fruit-pies in the galley for Hughie, who hated the fiddly job of cutting out the rounds of pastry, she thought that, despite the doctor's initial reaction, they were both settling down to work rather well together. He had taken her on deck earlier in the day to make notes, at his dictation, regarding the encroachment of ice up the measuring poles which had been set up, and had been almost pleasant over Sarah's wide-eyed pleasure in the amazing beauty of the ice which shimmered on the rigging, castled up the whaleback and formed icing-sugar palaces on the superstructure.

'It's so beautiful, but unbelievably cold,' she confided to Hughie, as she finished off the pastry rounds. 'I wasn't really convinced that a gull could die out there, but I am now!'

'I should hope so!' Hughie grinned affectionately at her across the floured table. 'And if you're so keen on the look of it out there, gal, you might go and 'ave another dekko and empty the galley slops at the same time.'

Emptying the left-over food and empty tins and bottles which Hughie gradually accumulated during the day was a task which the huge man detested and always passed over to someone else if he could. He was not built, he explained, for scrambling up the narrow companionway, nor for negotiating the iced-up, sloping deck to throw the rubbish to leeward.

'Righto, any excuse for a breath of fresh air,' Sarah said readily, reaching for her parka where it hung on the back of the galley door. She muffled herself up, then picked up the bucket, hefting it in both hands, for it was heavy. 'Shan't be long.'

She heaved the bucket along the corridor and up the companionway, then rested it on the top stair while she opened the door and slipped through. The deck was deserted and dim, lit only by the ship's riding lights, for the arcs were never turned on unless there was a party working outside.

Closing the door behind her she waited for a moment, to get accustomed to the temperature, then picked up the bucket again and staggered carefully over to the rail.

Having tipped the contents of the bucket into the heaving, sullen grey of the sea, she remained for a moment, leaning on the rail and gazing at the violent churning of the crests as they shouldered at the sides of the *Ice Venture*. She wished that she could see a whale, or some other sign that the Arctic sea was as full of creatures as the men insisted, but so far she had only seen birds, and they were growing fewer as the ship steamed north.

But only a few moments of watching the sea were enough to convince her that she would see nothing, not with the sea so turbulent, and the cold was biting, her muffler, steamed by her breath, was icing up. She would do better to go down below and ask one of the crew why it was that they never seemed to see any fish.

When the bucket was empty she had stood it down on the deck and now she made to pick it up, but found she could not do so since her mittens and the sleeves of her parka were frozen to the rail. She gave a snort of amusement at the foolishness of her plight and tried to step back so that she could heave more strongly against the grip of the ice on her clothing. She could not step back. Her boots were frozen to the deck!

Sarah panicked, feeling herself caught as helplessly by the ice as a fly in a spider's web. She turned her head as far as her position allowed and shouted at the top of her voice.

'Help! Help, someone, I'm iced up!'

But her voice was lost in the throb of the ship's engines and the howl of wind and waves.

She jerked again, fruitlessly, then again. The ice did not relax its grip by one hair's breadth, and now the cold was beginning to penetrate even through the thick parka so that her movements were perceptibly weaker. She told herself to keep calm and began to try to fight herself free of her coat and mittens, instead of just dragging against the ice. It was useless. The parka fitted her like a glove when worn over a number of thick sweaters and she dared not try to pull her feet out of her boots for she would still be anchored to the rail and would have little hope of reaching the safety of the companion-way even in the unlikely event of being able to wriggle out of all her outer clothing.

'Keep calm, Sarah,' she told herself, and heard the tremble in her voice. She called again, her voice no more than a seagull's mew, and muffled, further-more, by the thick woollen scarf around her face. The ice on the muffler was nearer to her mouth, she felt sure, insidiously creeping inwards as her breath cooled, slowed.

She knew, then, that the danger was real, that death could be terribly near. She was very afraid.

Tears formed in her eyes and ran down her cheeks, to freeze before they met the edge of her muffler into sparkling diamonds of ice. She wanted to give up, to sleep, to sag in her clothing across the rail and to let the cold do its worst.

She closed her eyes. Vaguely, she told herself that she ought to open them again at once, because the moisture on her lids would ice up and seal her sight into blackness, but she was so tired, so afraid. . .

She drifted into semi-consciousness, then into darkness.

CHAPTER THREE

SARAH came round to find herself draped over someone's shoulder, being carried at a great speed down some stairs. She moved a little and whimpered, because moving hurt, and a voice very near her ear said angrily: 'It's all right, you'll live. You'd better, so I can beat hell out of you for being such a little fool.'

The fury in his voice was strangely comforting, because, whoever he was, he cared enough to be angry with her. She could not immediately remember why anyone should be angry, but she hurt too much to waste time wondering how she had been hurt. She wondered more where she was, for when she opened her eyes she was inverted, with a view of an oil-skinned back, a linoleumed floor, and wooden bulkheads either . . .

Bulkheads! Of course, she was aboard the *Ice Venture*, and her rescuer was swerving into the nearest doorway. Her cabin, perhaps?

It was not her cabin. She found herself dumped unceremoniously down in a small, warm cubicle with tiled walls and floor and a dark blue plastic curtain which was being wrenched back. The showers? Yes, she was in one of the small shower cubicles.

Dr Rothwell steadied her with an arm round her shoulders, leaned over and turned the shower on, then began to take her parka off. Numbly, she noticed that she was not wearing her boots or mittens and remembered, suddenly, that she had been iced onto the rail and the deck by these garments. Someone must have lifted her out of the iced-up clothing and boots and brought her back here, and her mittens and footwear must still be attached to the ship! For some reason this worried her, in the illogical way in which small matters will suddenly loom enormous at times of stress.

'Wh-wh-where . . . b-b-boots . . . ?'

He lifted her up in one arm and took off her thick socks. Standing her down again, he made no attempt to answer her stuttered question, nor to glance at her, but began to deal with the rest of her garments, pulling off her two thick sweaters and the t-shirt with the slogan across the front. She heard him make some remark about the slogan, even registered the grin in his voice, but could not get her mind off her boots and mittens.

'My b-boots . . . M-my m-m-mittens . . . ?'

'Oh, your boots and mittens! I lifted you out of them, it was quicker than struggling to get them off the ice, but Don went up just now with a bucket of boiling water to unfreeze them and bring them below. Hold still, and I'll have you thawed in a brace of shakes.'

But she could not hold still, she was shivering and shuddering from top to toe and he was having difficulty with the fastening at the back of her bra . . . Her bra?

'Doctor! Oh, oh, oh! Stop it, s-stop it!'

Her voice was a wobbly pipe of outraged modesty, but Dr Rothwell, quite unperturbed, continued to remove her bra and to leave her only a pair of diminutive briefs, frilly and semi-transparent, as clothing.

'Don't be silly, please, Nurse Barford. I'm a doctor, you know, and just at the moment you're my patient, so start behaving like one! I've got to thaw you out, and quickly, so get under the shower and don't argue.'

He pushed her under the shower and needles of boiling hot water stung and pricked at her skin, flattening her long red hair into mermaid tresses, warming her blood back into brisk and painful circulation so that her eyes opened wide for the first time since her rescue.

The pain of returning feeling brought full consciousness back quicker than anything else could have done and, with it, understanding of her plight. She was in the shower cubicle with an angry Dr Rothwell, and she was as near naked as she could be. What was more, she was in agony, but every time she tried to escape from the hissing, stinging water he pushed her ruthlessly back beneath the stream, his eyes hard and humourless.

'Get back in the shower, my girl, until I'm satisfied that there's no frost left in you. Understand?'

Sobbing from the pain of her still sluggishly moving blood, she tried to tell him that she was all right now, must come out, while water fell into her eyes and her mouth so that her words came out as gurgles and her lashes, bedewed with drops, obscured her view of him, making it doubly difficult to elude his hands.

'Shut up and get—back—under!'

With every word he forced her back until she was once more fully immersed, her upper arms marked by his hands, her flesh glowing rosily from the needle-sharp impact of the hot water.

'I'm warm now! Please, sir, please . . .'

Her embarrassment and anxiety got through to him then, in a way she certainly did not intend, for his eyes, which had been fixed angrily on her face, dropped, to sweep across her rounded breasts with their rosy nipples, across the smooth skin of her stomach to the triangle of soaked nylon which was all her covering. And then he stepped into the shower with her, the water dancing unregarded on his dark head, soaking into the thick shetland wool sweater which covered his broad shoulders.

'Sarah?'

He gathered her into his arms, his hands moving over the long fall of heavy wet silk which was her hair, then pressing into the curve of her spine so that she was forced close as his gaze burned down into hers.

'Sarah?'

It was the merest whisper of her name before his mouth took hers, gently possessing, and suddenly she was on fire for him, nothing mattered but his hands, his mouth, the passion which had flowered in her at his touch, so that her arms crept round him, straining him close, and her lips softened and parted beneath his, as eager for his invasion as, two minutes earlier, she had feared it.

'Doc? Is she going to be all right?'

Don's voice, calling from outside the cubicle, brought them both out of whatever madness had possessed them. Dr Rothwell stepped back out of

the water. He was breathing hard and there was a
faint flush on his cheekbones, but his voice was rock
steady.

'She's starting to come round, but she's wet as a
fish and I've got pretty damp myself, so I'd be
grateful if you could sling a couple of towels over
the door.'

'Here they come. Anything else?'

Two thick orange towels appeared over the top
of the door.

'No, nothing else. Thanks very much.'

They heard Don leave the shower room and,
without a word, Dr Rothwell picked up Sarah's
thickest sweater and dragged it roughly over her
head, then wrapped a towel round her waist. It
reached her ankles and concealed the fact that she
was not wearing her cords.

'All right? Come on, then, I'll take you back to
your cabin.'

Sarah nodded, shivering again now, shocked out
of her desire for him by Don's voice, yet still
shatteringly aware of his reaction to her—and of
her own response.

What came over me? she thought with anguish as
she went before him towards her cabin. How could
I have flung myself into his arms like that? He had
started it, of course he had, but there could be no
denying the ardour of her response. To tell him that
she was not interested in men and then to behave
like a—a wanton! They reached her cabin door and
she became aware that he was looking down at her,
speaking to her. She forced herself to listen, to stop
reproaching herself for what had, after all, been
perhaps only the result of shock. She hoped he

would think so, anyway.

'. . . a hot drink, and you'll be fine by morning. I told Don to get hot-water bottles put into your bed, and you must pile on the extra blankets. I'll pop in in about an hour and if you can't sleep, I'll give you a shot of something, but I daresay exhaustion's the best sleeping drug at the moment.'

She gazed up at him, speechless. Not a word about what had happened in the shower, not so much as a softening of that hard, blue gaze!

'Go on, then!' He had opened the door and propelled her through it and now he followed her into the small room. 'Want me to tuck you up? And kiss you goodnight?'

There was a sardonic edge to his voice and she reacted at once, her chin lifting. How dared he mock her, after . . .

'No thank you, Doctor, and I don't n-need a hot drink or a sleeping draught. Goodnight!'

She waited. So did he. *Impasse!*

'Come along, Sarah, into bed with you!'

Sarah felt her face go hot. He could scarcely expect her to get into bed in a wet jersey and towel and he knew full well that she had nothing on underneath them.

'If you'll leave, I'll change into my pyjamas.'

He grinned, and she saw a glint in his eye which was a remembering glint. She swallowed, and felt her face go a shade hotter.

'Why? After all, I've seen . . .'

She flew across to the door and held it open, her hands shaking with rage.

'Get out!'

He walked slowly over to the door and, once

there, put out a hand and tilted her chin, then,
lightly, kissed her lips.

'Poor Sarah, I shouldn't tease you! Sleep well,
my child.'

He left, and she closed the door with a sound
perilously akin to a bang behind him, then made
her way back to the bed, feeling unaccountably
weak at the knees and also rather weepy. How
could he be so hateful? She really was in no fit state
to argue with him.

She stripped off the jersey and towel and dropped both disdainfully onto the floor. Let them lie
there! She was in no mood to bother about trifles
like crumpled clothing.

She dragged her nightie on over her head and
then, with some reluctance, got a cardigan out of
her drawer and put that on as well. She was still
shivering and weak, and knew, with the sensible
side of her mind, that she should do her utmost to
keep herself warm; that hot drink had been a good
idea and she had been a fool to fling it, so to speak,
back in Kurt Rothwell's face.

She climbed into bed and pulled up the covers,
snuggling well down and feeling the hot water
bottles at knee and toe level with considerable
pleasure. She realised, then, that she had not
turned the light out, and that she wanted, above
everything, to sleep, to forget the terror the ice had
wrought, and her foolishness in reacting to Dr
Rothwell's behaviour. She was nerving herself to
get out of bed, cross the floor and turn off the light
when the door opened after the briefest of knocks.

She glanced across the room, her hackless rising
even as her breathing quickened. How dared he

come back, when she had expressly said she did not want a hot drink, nor anything to help her to sleep. Yet, alongside that feeling, was another. Treacherously, her heartbeat quickened and her pulse leapt at the thought of him touching her, talking to her.

'I've brought you some cocoa, Sarah.' It was Hughie, tiptoeing into the room. 'And there's a tot of rum in it, to help you sleep.' He reached the bed and smiled down at her, concern obvious in his eyes. 'It's all right, I got the doc's permission; he said it was a good idea. And I'm going to sit with you until it's all finished, so's I can turn the light off, put an extra blanket or two on the bed, and generally see you comfortable.' He beamed at her, settling himself on the end of the bunk. 'I'm nurse for a bit, see?'

Unaccountably, Sarah felt tears rise to her eyes, and held out a hand for the mug of cocoa with fingers that were not quite steady. They were so kind to her! Even Dr Rothwell was not too bad—he had not snubbed Hughie's suggestion of rum in her cocoa to help her to sleep, nor had he told Hughie what a fool she had been. She had no doubt that she would be told by just about everyone aboard in the fullness of time, but the moment had not yet come. They would let her recover first.

'Thanks, Hughie.' She sipped at the drink. 'Oh, it's lovely!'

Ten minutes later, when Hughie let himself quietly out of her cabin, she was already fast asleep.

She awoke next morning to find Hughie beaming at her around her half-open door.

'Feeling better, gal? Good! I've brought you a

nice cuppa and a few biscuits, and doc says to tell you, when you're fit, he's in the sickbay. He said to let you sleep in until now, because all that ailed you was tiredness.' He tiptoed heavily across the floor, the mug of tea held out before him like a votive offering. 'Here we are, then!'

'You're so kind, Hughie,' Sarah said, leaning up on her elbow and sipping the tea. 'I could eat a horse!'

'Got eggs and bacon in the galley, all ready for the pan,' Hughie offered. 'Be there in ten minutes, can you?'

'For eggs and bacon, anything!'

'You're on, gal!' Hughie made for the door. 'Don't try to rush, now.'

As she put on her uniform, Sarah found herself getting quite indignant over Dr Rothwell's behaviour of the previous day. To be sure, she had been silly and he had undoubtedly saved her life, but he had been, she reminded herself, *very* unethical. To tell her in one breath that she was a patient and in the next to try to seduce her—well, that was not at all the way a doctor should behave.

The trouble was that there was no way she could accuse him without setting her own pulse racing at the recollection of those lean hands smoothing down her bare back, dragging her ruthlessly close. For him, of course, it had been different—men were opportunists, each and every one. He had seized the chance offered by proximity and her dazed state, but by now he had probably forgotten the feel of her beneath his hands, the way her mouth tasted, whereas she . . .

Sarah chided herself and strained her hair back into a ponytail so severe that her eyebrows were tightened and her forehead felt stiff. Then she marched out of the door and along to the galley. To her relief, Hughie was alone, handling a massive frying pan in which eggs and bacon sizzled.

'Well done, gal! Eat that up, and you'll be fit to face a tiger!'

He doled out a generous portion of eggs, bacon and fried bread onto a plate and slapped it down before Sarah, now seated at the galley table. Sarah, taking an ecstatic mouthful, raised her brows at him.

'Face a tiger?'

'A figure of speech, gal.' Hughie reddened and glanced sideways at her. 'I daresay you've guessed that it was daft to 'ang about on the deck, and the doc can be quick-tempered. He might feel he has to say a word or two.'

Sarah grinned with a jauntiness she was far from feeling.

'Oh, I see! I'll eat up and be brave then. After all, anyone can make a mistake.'

'Not on a trawler, gal. One mistake can be your last.'

'I know it.' Sarah sighed and ate in silence for a moment, then pushed her empty plate away and stood up. 'Thanks for a lovely meal, Hughie. I'll go and face that tiger now!'

She entered the sickbay with quick, almost defiant steps, knowing that as Dr Rothwell turned to face her warmth was spreading slowly across her cheeks, but trying to tell herself that if he really let fly at her, she would tell him what she thought of his unethical behaviour. However, she had underestimated her adversary.

'This man Evans, Nurse! You gave him a anti-tetanus injection?'

Puzzled, Sarah nodded.

'Yes, I did, because the wounds on his fingers were deep, and I thought . . .'

'You thought! Tell me, Sarah, are you or are you not a fully trained, experienced, state registered nurse?'

Sarah tightened her lips at his sarcastic inflection but nodded, her eyes fixed on his face.

'Yet it did not occur to you to ask the man whether he had had an ATT within the last five years?'

'Well, no, I assumed . . .'

'You assume nothing in medicine, Nurse. According to the treatment book you made no provision for a second injection after six weeks, nor a third after six months.'

'Well, no, I thought he'd probably had an ATT some time in the last two years. I thought I was giving him a booster.'

'Why should you think that? Were you not taught, in hospital, to get a doctor's permission before giving an ATT? Before treating a patient, in fact?'

'Yes I was, b-but you said I was to deal with wh-whatever happened so you c-could get on with your w-work,' stammered Sarah, her face on fire. 'I th-thought, in a job like his . . .'

Dr Rothwell slammed the treatment book down on the desk with such force that Sarah jumped.

'Nurse Barford, under no circumstances should

you give a patient an injection of any description when a doctor is within call. All you had to do was *ask*, damn it. I've not laid down hard and fast rules because there may come a time when you simply must use your own initiative, but if so, make sure that the patient tells you his history before you do *anything*. Is that clear?'

'Yes, sir. I'm sorry.'

'Very well. And since I'm finding fault, never go on deck again alone, and never lean on the rail for more than a few seconds. Clear?'

Sarah's face felt hot enough to roast chestnuts on, and she could not meet his eyes, but she nodded vigorously, so that he would not think her sulky.

'Yes, sir.'

'Good. Now the whole subject is closed.' He came round from behind the desk and handed her a sheaf of notes. 'Get these typed up, please. I'm going out on deck with Alan, to see how much krill he's netted.'

He was gone before she could comment, closing the door firmly behind him. Sarah walked slowly round the desk, pulled out the portable typewriter, and sat down in front of it, then threaded a sheet of paper around the roller.

It was not until she had typed quite half his notes that it suddenly occurred to her that he had quite probably brought up the business of the anti-tetanus injection so that she could not make any accusations about what had happened in the shower the previous day. She had not been allowed to open her mouth, now she thought about it, and he had made sure that she never did open it on that particular subject, by following a monumental telling-off with the strict injunction not to mention either subject again.

She pondered the matter for a moment, her initial indignation gradually waning. All in all, they had brushed through the business very well. It was far better to forget it and work together as though they had never fallen into each other's arms and clung passionately beneath the pattering water.

Only forgetting it would not be so easy.

Not for her.

CHAPTER FOUR

FOR several days, the working relationship between Sarah and Dr Rothwell continued cautiously amicable, though since he rarely came onto the mess deck in the evenings, when relaxation was the order of the day, she could scarcely begin to form a more personal relationship with him, as she was beginning to do with other members of the team.

She soon got to know and like most of the men with whom she worked. She began to regard them quite differently, too, for the married men—Stan, Albert, Fred and Don—treated her far more naturally and easily than did the bachelors. That was not to say, of course, that the married men did not flirt with her and tease her, but the manner in which they did so was far less intense than the manner in which Alan and Phil tended to behave.

However, with the start of the day-long, night-long dark, things began to settle into a definite routine aboard the *Ice Venture*. Dr Rothwell instigated a clinic from nine till eleven each morning when he and Sarah attended to injuries, prescribed for minor ailments, and generally looked after the well-being of team and crew, beside doing standard tests and correlating the information thus obtained.

From eleven until twelve-thirty, Sarah usually went to the galley to help Hughie with the preparation of lunch, and during the afternoons she typed up Dr Rothwell's reports and did any filing or other office work that might have accrued. There were other diversions, if such they could be called. Several times, the captain invited Sarah onto the bridge to see for herself the vicious weather conditions under which trawlermen worked, and to be shown how the radar worked, to talk on the radio to other distant-water trawlers within range, and to watch the echo sounder, ceaselessly drawing a picture of the sea bed.

Her trips up on deck, however, were severely limited, both by the viciousness of the weather and by the constant dark. She could only go on deck when the arc-lights illuminated it, and the arc lights were only switched on when men were working out there, which meant that trips to empty rubbish or just to gaze out at that vast and lonely ocean had to be made at certain times and not simply when it was convenient for her.

But though she did not see as much of Kurt Rothwell in the evenings as she did of the rest of the team, she found out quite a lot about him from the casual conversation around her. He was not married, though he appeared to have had some stunningly beautiful girlfriends, and he was generally regarded as one who had women perpetually chasing him—particularly nurses.

'Well, he need have no fear as far as *I'm* concerned,' Sarah said when she heard this. 'He's met one nurse who's absolutely impervious to his so-called charms. He's too bossy by half, to say nothing of being convinced that he's always right!

'Oh, you'll fall for him in the end, they all do,' Stan said teasingly. He knew Kurt Rothwell better, probably, than anyone else, since he and Kurt had worked together before.

'What, with *me* around?' Alan Wilde was fair-haired and handsome, with a Grecian profile and a magnificent physique. 'Rothwell hasn't got a hope!'

'To be fair, he dislikes me as much as I dislike him,' Sarah said. 'I'm perfectly sure that hoping about me goes no further than hoping I don't drop another thermometer.'

There was a shout of laughter from Phil, who had happened to be in the sickbay when Sarah had dropped, in quick succession, a glass measuring jug, a medicine bottle and a thermometer, and had had the doubtful privilege of hearing Dr Rothwell's unexpurgated view of clumsy nurses.

'Don't underestimate yourself, Sarah. Kurt's the sort that can shout one minute and kiss the next, I daresay.'

'Not me, he can't,' Sarah said, pursing her lips. 'I want to marry a millionaire when I settle down, not a doctor.'

'Who said anything about marriage?'

'And I'm old-fashioned, and a prude,' Sarah said promptly, making Phil laugh again. 'And now I'm going to bed, so you can continue this discussion without me.'

Despite the episode over the breakages, which had happened during a storm and which Sarah still felt had not been her fault, Dr Rothwell's opinion of her was high enough to let her take the clinic now without his presence. She was doing so one morning, renewing a dressing on an ice-burn, when Alan and Don burst in, looking very pleased with themselves.

'Sarah, come on deck. You know we put the trawl down this morning, early, despite the old man saying it was a poor place for fish? Well, you must see what we've caught!'

That was Alan, hair on end, face flushed.

'Oh, Alan, how can I? I'm doing the clinic.'

Alan consulted his wristwatch, not without difficulty, for he was muffled up in his outdoor gear and had to remove his mittens before he could get at his watch.

'Why? It's eleven-fifteen.' He grinned at the crew member with the ice-burn. 'Don't you know better than to injure yourself after eleven o'clock? The girl's off duty now.'

The crew member examined his neat new dressing and then turned to Sarah.

'Go on, Nurse, go with the lads! It's probably nothing much, but you'll get no peace unless you do, and my 'and's just fine now.'

'All right, Thomas, I'll go and have a look. Curiosity is very much part of my makeup, unfortunately. And keep the dressing dry this time, if you can manage it.' She turned to the men. 'Pass me my outdoor gear, then.'

Five minutes later they made their way on deck, with Alan leading and Don holding her arm.

'Look!' Alan pointed to where the trawl net was still swaying above the deck. 'Have you ever seen uglier blighters?'

'Catfish,' the doctor's voice said quietly, near Sarah's ear. 'Not pretty, I agree.'

'They're horrible,' Sarah agreed, watching the huge fish apprehensively as they squirmed and fought in the net. 'They look vicious, too. Can you eat them? I've never heard of fried catfish!'

'In fish cakes and fish fingers, who knows what they're eating?' countered Alan, gesturing to the men on the trawl to release the catch into the fish pens. 'It'll help to defray the cost of the expedition if we can take home some fish to sell.'

'I suppose . . .' began Sarah, and just as she spoke one of the fish flipped, lunged, and landed right at her feet. Sarah felt herself seized round the waist and dragged to safety just as Stan, with his back to the fish pen, stepped backwards, cannoning into Alan who had also jumped out of the way of the writhing fish. Stan fell heavily, with one arm bent under him, Alan went over to the other man, and a crew member strode across the deck and kicked the fish back into the catch pen.

It all happened so quickly that Sarah was scarcely set down on her feet again before Dr Rothwell seemed to have diagnosed the situation.

'Sarah, get back to the clinic, fast!' he rapped, striding over to Stan. 'Give me a hand, chaps, that arm's fractured, or I'm a Dutchman!'

Sarah shot ahead of the small party helping Stan. She had barely got her outdoor clothing off when the door opened and Stan and his two assistants— for the others had obviously realised they were not needed when it came to the narrow companion-way—entered the room. Dr Rothwell settled the patient in a chair and gently eased him out of his duffelcoat, then surveyed the injured arm. Even to Sarah, who had done very little time in Casualty, the diagnosis was obvious.

'Colles' fracture,' Dr Rothwell remarked, while poor Stan, white as a sheet, looked apprehensively

at his arm, pushed right out of shape by the fall.
'What's the other name for it, Sarah?'

'Dinner-fork fracture, sir,' Sarah said promptly.
'And you can see why, Stan.'

'Well, it's fortunate as it happens, because we
can cope with this without too much bother,' the
doctor said, patting Stan's shoulder. 'Isn't that
right, Nurse?'

'Yes, of course,' Sarah said, with a confidence
she was far from feeling. She knew all about Colles'
fractures in theory, but as luck would have it she
had never actually nursed one. However, she bore
in mind the doctor's recent strictures on patients
finding out that they were to be guinea pigs, and
just hoped that she might have an opportunity to
confess to Dr Rothwell before she was actually
asked to do anything.

'Alan, stay here, we'll need a third pair of hands.
No, on second thoughts, nip up to the Bond cupboard and bring down a bottle of rum, would you?
Better ask the captain first, I suppose.' As Alan left
the room the doctor turned to Sarah. 'Here a
minute, Nurse.'

Sarah approached, tying the strings of her apron
as she did so.

'Here I am, sir. Shall I start getting Stan's upper
clothing off? We'll need the sweaters off, to plaster
it later, and . . .'

'That's the idea.' He turned to Stan. 'Look, bite
your lip old chap, we'll want all that clothing off and
it may be a bit painful, that's why I think we'll let
Sarah do it. She'll be gentler than I would.'

However, it took both of them to ease the heavy
sweaters and the shirt off Stan's lean form without

touching the injured arm, and though the sweat stood out on the patient's brow at the finish, Sarah suspected he had not been nearly as nervous as she. However, at last Stan was down to his singlet and, with Alan's return, they could begin.

'Right. Nurse, get some disposable syringes, please. I'll want Pethidine, Ativan and Lignocaine. And when it's all done, I'll pour Stan a double, to celebrate. Well, I shall if I've clicked the bone into alignment, at any rate.'

Sarah, watching Stan, saw him turn green at this mention of clicking bones, and directed a reproving glare at Kurt Rothwell. After all his talk about giving the patients confidence, too!

'You won't feel a thing, Stan, that's why Dr Rothwell got me to fetch all these syringes. Here we are, sir,' she pushed the trolley forward, laden with all that he would need, 'I think that's the lot.'

Dr Rothwell's glance swept the trolley, then he nodded.

'Seems all right. Now Stan, this'll ease matters.' He injected the injured arm, then turned to Sarah. 'Cuff please, Nurse.'

Sarah adjusted the b.p. cuff round the top of Stan's arm and pumped it up.

'At 240 please, Nurse. And hold it at that.'

Sarah adjusted the sphyg. until it read 240 and then nodded to the doctor.

'Steady on 240, sir.'

'Good.' Another injection, then he chatted idly to Stan. Sarah guessed that he was waiting for the Lignocaine to take effect. Presently, he caught hold of the injured arm at the wrist. Stan, who happened to be looking over his shoulder at Alan, never even blinked.

Kurth Rothwell spoke quietly, keeping his eyes on his patient's countenance.

'Alan, take a good grip on the upper part of Stan's arm, please. I shall take his hand and pull until the bone clicks back into place. Sarah will keep the cuff blown up to 240.' He turned back to Stan, who, reassured by the numbness of his lower arm, was a better colour and showing no signs of his previous nervousness. 'You can watch if you like, or you can feast your eyes on the lovely nurse there. This takes strength, but you won't feel a thing. Now, Alan!'

Sarah watched as the two men indulged in a tug of war, with Stan's arm as the rope. Sweat beaded their foreheads before, with an audible click, Stan's arm yielded to *force majeure* and allowed itself to be tugged straight.

'Phew!' It was Stan who exclaimed, but Sarah could see that the other men, too, were glad the ordeal was over. 'I say, look at that! It's not at all bent, it's as right as rain!'

'Yes, but you've got to get plastered or it won't stay that way,' Sarah said, slowly releasing the b.p. cuff and watching the indicator sink. 'I'll fetch *my* equipment now.'

Stan grinned and pointed to the rum bottle.

'That, do you mean? Go on, doc, Sarah just said I must get plastered, so hand over the bottle!'

'You can have one when it's all over; not long now.' Dr Rothwell brought over a bucket of water from the sink and stood it down by Sarah so that she could use it for her plastering. 'Alan and I could do with a snorter too, after all that tugging!'

'If you've finished with me, I'll go back up on deck,' Alan said. 'I'll have my drink later.' He made for the door. 'Sure there's nothing else?'

'No, we can manage now, thanks.' Dr Rothwell walked over to where Sarah was carefully folding cottonwool round the injured arm and then beginning to apply the plaster bandages. He watched for a moment, presumably to make sure that she was competent to do the job, then went over and began to rummage amongst Stan's discarded clothing.

'You won't be able to wear sweaters until the plaster's dry,' he remarked presently. 'Have you a loose jacket or something? If so, I'll fetch it for you while Sarah finishes the plastering.'

'Yup. In the bottom drawer in my cabin there's a lumberjacket with quite wide sleeves. That's what you mean, isn't it?'

'That's right. What colour is it?'

'Black and red checks,' Stan said, grinning at Sarah. 'The sort of thing everyone wears in the backwoods. You can't miss it, Kurt.'

'Right, I'll get it. Nearly finished, Nurse?'

Sarah smoothed the last bandage on, then stood up, stripping off her rubber gloves.

'Yes, just done, sir. Shall I fetch the jacket?'

'No, you've got to clear up.' He jerked his head at the rum bottle. 'Pour Stan a small one while I'm gone.'

'Don't you dare!' Stan said as soon as the door closed behind the doctor. 'Pour me a very large one. After all, that was what Kurt said when he was persuading me to sit still and shut up!'

'True.' Sarah poured a small drink, then added a

little more. 'Want water in it?'

'No! That's sacrilege, woman!' He eyed the glass in a dissatisfied manner as she held it out. 'Is that a double? You've barely wet the glass.'

'Well, he *did* say a double.' Sarah splashed another measure recklessly into the glass. 'Just drink it up and don't tell the doctor, because you may be sure I'd get blamed.'

'I won't.' Stan gulped the rum in one draught, then blinked. 'Cor, that's made my toes curl! Put your monicker on my plaster, gorgeous, and I'll go and rest for a bit. Strangely enough, I can't raise much enthusiasm for deckwork today.'

Sarah began to clear round Stan, pushing the trolley back by the sink and brushing the floor.

'Mustn't sign plaster for twenty-four hours, but then I might jot down my name and number. You'll want a sling, Stan, but I can't give you one until the doctor comes back with your jacket. And don't go splashing around and getting the plaster wet, there's a dear. You've got to let the bone set, and it can't do that if it's always being re-plastered. A friend of mine once had a little patient—mad on horses she was—and she had four Colles' fractures running. She was a little devil, hitting her brothers with the plaster, diving into the bath with it on, and the last time she fractured it, it healed bent. So be warned!'

'I'll be careful. I'll get someone else to muck about with Alan's plankton, if that's what you're thinking of,' Stan said.

'There you are! You can't go on deck in all weathers with that plaster on your arm. You'll have to take it easy.'

'I'm going to do my own work,' Stan protested, staring up at her. 'No way can I sit round doing nothing.'

'I'll let Dr Rothwell lecture you, he's far better at it than I,' Sarah said, carrying her plaster bucket back to the sink.

'Oh, don't worry, Kurt'll understand that I can't stop work,' Stan assured her. 'Kurt knows how important it is that . . .'

'What was that, Stan?'

Dr Rothwell, entering quietly with the jacket in one hand, looked enquiringly across at Stan.

'Oh, nothing, Kurt, only Sarah was trying to tell me I couldn't work, and I was assuring her that you know only too well how important it is that I . . .'

'How important it is that a fracture is allowed to mend,' Dr Rothwell finished blandly. 'Yes, Nurse Barford is absolutely right. You must keep your arm in the sling that she is about to prepare . . . yes, I see you are, Sarah there's no need to pinch your lips together quite so righteously . . . and you won't do any deckwork for at least ten days. Then we'll see how things go.'

'But Kurt, I won't *use* the arm! Surely it can't hurt for me to walk about the deck, supervise . . .' Stan said anxiously. 'All my work, my experiments . . .'

'Rest assured they'll be done. You must write down what you want doing each day and I'll see that it's performed.' He turned, to eye Sarah thoughtfully. 'Sarah can manage! She can do your deckwork instead of helping Hughie in the galley in the mornings. Yes, an excellent idea! Nurse Barford will do your bidding.'

Sarah, helping Stan into his jacket, patted his shoulder. 'I'll do it willingly, Stan. As for Hughie,' she cast a speaking glance at Dr Rothwell, 'I'm sure he can manage very well without me.'

Stan glanced pathetically from one to the other.

'But I could go on deck! Just to see that Sarah's doing things the way I want them done. I wouldn't interfere, but . . .'

'You'd bulldoze the girl into letting you work,' Dr Rothwell said firmly. 'No use crying over spilt milk, Stan, that arm's got to have a chance to mend and I *am*, as you seem to forget, leading this expedition. Kindly do as you're told.'

Stan left the room looking extremely cast down and Sarah began to clean the floor, her lips tight.

'What's the matter, swallowed a lemon?' enquired Kurt Rothwell in his most affable voice. 'Or is your housemaid's knee killing you?'

Sarah shot him a fulminating look from under her brows. She was on her hands and knees now, mopping up the splashes of plaster.

'Sarah will do your bidding,' she mimicked crossly. 'You must know that the moment Stan's mobile again he'll keep nipping up on deck and there won't be a thing I can do to stop him.'

'I said Nurse Barford, not Sarah,' Dr Rothwell pointed out, smiling condescendingly down at her. 'I'm always formal when we're in a formal situation, or hadn't you noticed? As for managing Stan, of course you can! Think of all those patients in the male surgical ward who obeyed you implicitly for two years. You had no trouble with them, you told me so yourself when I wondered at your abilities in that direction.'

'Yes, but they were in bed, and . . .' Sarah's voice died away as his grin spread.

'Precisely what I said! But my dear girl, Stan's only got to be threatened with me and he'll behave himself. Believe it or not, none of the men want to get into my bad books because they want to be included in other expeditions I lead, and they know they won't be picked again if they disobey orders now.'

'I see.' Sarah got up from her knees and went to put her floor cloth back in the bucket. 'Well, how do you hope to control me, then, because I don't for one moment delude myself that you'd take me on another expedition?'

'You're a trained nurse, my dear girl, and trained nurses, like trained dogs, obey their masters. Force of habit.'

Sarah swung round, intending to leave the room, but he caught hold of her and swung her back to face him. He was laughing, but there was a challenge in the bright eyes which looked lazily down into hers.

'Don't just rush out of the room when you're losing an argument. Of course you obey a doctor, and so you should.'

Sarah tried to jerk herself out of his grip. She was angry, and it showed in the bright colour in her cheeks.

'You really despise nurses, don't you? You think we're all good for nothing but obeying the commands of the nearest doctor, whatever they may happen to be! Well, it's rubbish, because I've nursed on wards where the sisters and nurses protect inadequate doctors from the results of their own stupidity, and where nurses take decisions which doctors have opted out of. So there!'

He pulled her closer, and she dropped the cloth she was holding but kept her angry eyes on his face. How dared he as good as call her a trained poodle! And how dare he continue to laugh down at her when she was being as rude as she knew how.

'Temper improves you, Sarah. You look eminently kissable when you're indignant.' His fingers tightened. 'Shall I put it to the test?'

'I don't think I would if I were you,' Sarah muttered through gritted teeth. She could feel her heartbeats quickening at his nearness, and she had no desire whatsoever to find herself melting into his arms. He was quite conceited enough without realising what a devastating effect he had on her!

'But you aren't me.' He pulled her right into his arms, so that she was pressed against his broad chest, unable to look up at him without tilting her chin back. She swallowed, staring straight before her at the top button on his white coat. 'Sarah? Look up, chick! This is a scientific experiment!'

'I am neither a chick nor a trained dog. Let me go!' Sarah pushed against his chest with both hands. 'Really, doctor, you're just proving my point up to the hilt. You despise me, or you'd allow me the dignity of choice.'

Rather to her surprise, he released her at once, and turned away, walking briskly over to the desk.

'Very well, if that's how you feel. And if you want to know the real reason that you do as you're told, it's because you want a decent reference out of me when this trip's over, and you know you won't get one by disobeying.' He turned, to eye her coldly. All the laughter, the friendship, had gone from his glance. 'As for despising nurses, I certainly do no such thing. I've known too many excellent and efficient ones to make such an error. As for you, personally, I believe that you'll prove efficient as well, given time, so you may well get a good reference, despite our personal feelings.'

Sarah took a deep breath. She had antagonised him this time, and found herself very much wishing she had not.

'I'm sorry. I'm afraid you caught me on the raw. But don't think I'm apologising because I want a good reference, because I don't think it will make the slightest difference. After all, this has only been a very short interlude, and I needn't even mention it when applying for my next job. As you know, I got very good references from my last hospital.'

'I thought you hoped for a job on a cruise ship? I could help with that, you know.'

'Perhaps,' Sarah said rather uneasily. He had turned back and was standing rather too close, looking down at her with a half-smile on his lips. 'But I'd rather get such a job off my own bat.'

'Independent! But remember that I know most of the people who want nursing staff for unusual jobs. A word here and there that you were too independent, could keep you out in the cold!'

Sarah moved sideways, then bent down to pick up the fallen cloth. When she straightened she went past him to the sink, not wanting to be trapped against the door again.

'I'm sure you wouldn't give way to a desire to talk about me adversely unless I gave you good cause,' Sarah said over her shoulder. 'And I shan't give you good cause, because I really am good at my job. What about Stan? Will he need painkillers when the Lignocaine wears off?'

'If he does, I'll see to it.' He moved over to the door which led into his office. 'There'll be some typing for you in about twenty minutes.'

'I'll come back then. I'm just going to give Hughie a hand.' She waited, but he said nothing, so she slipped out into the corridor, closing the door softly behind her. Then she blew out her cheeks in a long whistle of relief.

Phew, she never knew where she was with Kurt Rothwell! Sometimes he was like any other man, only more so, and his touch made her pulses race. But at other times he was horrible; sarcastic, threatening, difficult. She was still sure that she had been right when she had accused him of despising nurses. And the threats which he had undoubtedly made, of passing the word around that she was not right for special work, had been rather uncalled for. Oh, she had been rude, but that was no reason to virtually blacklist her!

She walked down to the galley, where she found Hughie busy with his lunch preparations. Pans steamed, food was already laid out on some plates, and he was moving round his tiny galley with his usual ponderous authority.

Nice Hughie, Sarah thought, with a sudden rush of affection. He could joke with her and order her about and never did she sense that antagonism which sometimes seemed to emanate from Kurt Rothwell. As for making her do the deckwork in the time she usually spent in the galley, she would try and manage Stan better than that. Dr Rothwell knew she enjoyed being with Hughie, and had probably chosen that time deliberately. But she would prove to him that she could cope with Stan, with Stan's work and with her cooking as well.

CHAPTER FIVE

IN FACT, Stan's injury did have a bright side, for Sarah if not for Stan himself. It varied her days. To be sure she had to work much harder, but now at least she got out on deck with the other team members. Stan explained patiently exactly what he wanted done, and she carried out his wishes to the best of her ability. But perhaps happiest of all was the fact that Stan, bored by being so much alone, volunteered to help her with the typing and filing work which needed doing. She knew that the doctor, if he found out, would not have been best pleased, but she never let Stan type anything that was even slightly confidential and on the more straightforward stuff he was a great help, though his one-handed, two-fingered typing was, of necessity, somewhat slow and laborious.

Stan's work was interesting, varied, and it brought her fresh air and company, and his help meant that she could enjoy the extra work, instead of being battered to her knees by the sheer volume of tasks expected of her.

There were times when she saw Dr Rothwell watching her with an expression of reluctant admiration, and then she smiled to herself, but was careful to say nothing to give the game away. After all, she was working harder than almost anyone else aboard, and Stan's work on the typewriter hurt no one, but she never knew how Dr Rothwell would react, and she had no intention of rocking the boat by letting him discover that she had a helper.

Clinic time, too, was enlivened by Stan. Dr Rothwell was a good enough psychiatrist as well as a good enough doctor to realise that Stan must do something to while away the hours, and he raised no objection to Stan helping at the clinic, though sometimes Sarah, glancing at her boss, surprised a look in his eyes which she knew well, and thought that he would be very relieved when Stan was busy with his own work again and not pottering around the clinic.

However, there had been no more storms since the brief but furious one after Stan's arm had been plastered. She was learning that the best way to behave with Dr Rothwell was to get quietly on with her work, and to try to have a third person present when they were together. This, it seemed, made him think twice about either finding fault or making passes—and both, she told herself firmly, were equally distasteful.

Then, one morning about five days after Stan's fracture, she and Alan Wilde were on deck together checking anonometer readings, ice encroachment, and temperatures. They would also bring up Alan's drag net. This object skimmed the surface of the ocean and gathered up all sorts of animal and vegetable matter which smelt strange, but Alan treated it like gold-dust and was always singing its praises as a possible food source for the poor and penniless.

'It may be all right if you're poor and penniless,

have no sense of smell and don't mind the taste of codliver oil,' Stan moaned, having been persuaded to taste some. 'Did you say the Japanese eat it, Alan? Aren't they the ones who eat ants in chocolate and bumble bees? Well, my God, no wonder!'

Rightly guessing from his words that plankton was not to his taste, Sarah prudently refused Alan's invitations to have a mouthful, but she always enjoyed seeing the catch brought up. So many shapes, such weird little creatures!

This particular day was a wild one. Because of the pitch dark, Sarah always had difficulty in realising, on deck, that it was in fact day. The arc-lights, she felt, only served to emphasise their tininess in the great, Arctic world of ocean which tumbled in the foam around the ship. She and Alan often helped one another with their deckwork, and now she struggled with him to the anonometer, situated in the partial shelter of the whaleback. Stan, at first, had been scornful of anything which had to be tucked out of the way of the gales which blew— 'How can I measure the wind's force if my anonometer is out of the wind?' he had asked plaintively—but having had his instrument blown down a couple of times and hurled right across into the scuppers once, he had consented to at least a partial sheltering.

Now, bent double against the wind, Alan read the figures aloud at the top of his voice whilst Sarah wrote them down. The ice-encroachment, however, proved to be more difficult.

'Where are the measuring poles?' Alan roared against the wind. Sarah looked and spotted them— well under the ice. She pointed them out to Alan, who grinned and made a gesture indicative of impotence. It was true that no way could they measure how far the ice had encroached up the poles today.

However, there was still work to do. Alan beckoned and they both leaned over the ship's side and began to pull his drag net inboard. They had it up, level with the rail, when the heavy sea caught the *Ice Venture* at a disadvantage and tipped her at an angle. Sarah and Alan, caught unawares and with the weight of the net further unbalancing them, went hurtling across the deck like ninepins struck by a successful ball. They cannoned into the door of the forward locker, which gave beneath their combined weight and caved inwards, letting them and the drag net shoot through into the interior where they lay, hopelessly entangled, amongst the fishing tackle and netting which the locker contained.

Sarah, sitting up, stared into the darkness.

'Alan? Are you all right?'

She realised as she spoke that it was dark because the door of the locker must have swung shut as suddenly as it had swung open.

'I think so. But I've got plankton porridge down my neck, inside my boots . . . hell, I'm giving up for today! Let's go back indoors and clean ourselves up.' There was not sufficient height for him to stand but she heard him crawling over to the door. 'I'll just give the door . . . Oh, no! Oh, hell!'

'What's the matter?' Sarah, too, crawled towards where the door must be. 'Give it a shove, it's horrible in here!'

Alan groaned, then sat down with a thump.

'The bloody door's gone and locked itself! It opens inwards, of course, and since people aren't supposed to go into lockers, there's nothing on this side of the door to open it with.'

'Oh, no!' Sarah reached the door and felt frantically across its smooth surface. 'This can't happen to me! Dr Rothwell will be livid, he wanted me to type up all his reports on the last medical he gave the crew. If we bang and shout, won't someone hear us?'

'We could try. But there was no one else on deck, was there?'

'No, the others had all finished and gone below. But we'll be missed. Dr Rothwell will go into the sickbay—well, no, perhaps he won't, but Stan . . . oh *damn*, Stan was helping in the fishroom. Alan, won't someone miss you?'

'I doubt it. Not until dinner time. What's the time, do you know?'

Sarah peered in vain at her tiny wristwatch.

'Don't know, this thing isn't luminous. But it must be about half-three, I should think.'

Alan groaned.

'Half past three! It's another three hours before we shall be missed, then. Dear God, we could be dead of the cold in that time.'

He moved nearer to Sarah. She could feel his warm breath on her cheek, and she moved closer to him, too. Just to have another person present, she reflected, was a comfort in a situation like this.

'But we aren't on the open deck, and we've got coats and mufflers on. We couldn't die of cold. Could we?'

Alan laughed shortly.

'Not if we huddle close together, but we'll be pretty cold and miserable in three hours. Well, come here.' He pulled her close, his arms closing around her. 'What shall we do to pass the time?'

His arm manoeuvred her until his mouth could seek hers. Sarah pushed him sharply.

'Not that! We'll play quiz games though, if you like.'

Alan nuzzled the side of her face and got another shove. He sighed, but moved back a little.

'If you insist, though what I was about to suggest would have warmed us up much better!'

'It might have warmed you,' Sarah said acidly, 'but it wouldn't have warmed me. It would take more than you to do that!'

'The original ice maiden, eh?' Alan chuckled. 'You really are Arctic, Nurse!' His arms were still round her, but she knew that he would not attempt to force his attentions on her, not when they were in such an uncomfortable predicament at any rate. She relaxed against him, grateful for his good sense and humour.

'Look, let's play Twenty Questions. I'll start.'

Alan sighed and released her to kneel up for a moment, close to the door.

'I never thought I'd find myself shut in the dark with a beautiful woman, playing Twenty Questions! My friends back home will never believe it! So for my pride's sake, I'm going to bash on this door a few times with a chunk of whatever this thing is, coal I think, and see if anyone comes.'

Outside they could hear the roar of the waves and the howling of the wind. Knowing that it was useless, Sarah joined him, and they both banged and shouted.

Then, sitting back on their heels, they listened.

Wind and waves. The throb of the engines sounding almost like a purr against the elements. Alan sat down and reached out and tugged her into his arms again.

'No use. Let's keep close and share what warmth there is and hope for a speedy discovery. Now if you're going to start, is your object animal, vegetable or mineral? We won't have that other one, we'll stick to those three. Fire ahead!'

Ages later, when they had grown heartily tired of Twenty Questions, I Spy (played from memory of the mess deck, since the locker remained obstinately pitch-black) and Quotations, they heard voices through the door, raised against the elements.

'They're searching for us!' Sarah shrieked. She was opening her mouth to shriek again when the door suddenly shot open and a torch was played across her face.

'Come out of that!'

Dr Rothwell's voice was even colder than the interior of the locker. Alan seemed to notice nothing but began to crawl towards freedom, courteously pushing Sarah ahead of him, telling their rescuers what an ordeal they had suffered and how it had come about.

Don was with the doctor and he replied, telling how they had imagined, for one awful moment, that the missing ones had been washed overboard until Dr Rothwell had suddenly thought of the locker.

'I can tell you, the relief when we opened the door was tremendous,' he told them as they crossed the deck to go below into warmth and safety once more. But Sarah could sense not relief but positive fury emanating from the doctor's well-muffled form.

At the foot of the companionway, Alan turned to her and threw a careless arm round her shoulders.

'Well, beautiful, ordeal over! I'll see you at dinner.'

Sarah, with a quick glance at Dr Rothwell's countenance, muttered something. Retribution was plainly at hand and she was in no mood for it. If the doctor started on her for getting locked into the forward locker by accident, she really would tell him a thing or two. She enjoyed typing up the medical sheets, and nothing would have made her go to such elaborate lengths to avoid the work.

But this, it appeared, was not what was making Kurt Rothwell look like thunder. As soon as they were in the sickbay, he disabused her mind on that score.

'Nurse Barford, I warned you right from the start that I'd have no flirting or carrying on with the men, and then I find you locked in a very small space with one of the most sex-hungry young men it has been my misfortune to meet. You were so full of your ability to control men, to cope with everything, that I must conclude you were a willing partner in whatever went on, and frankly, Nurse, it isn't good enough. What sort of trust can I place in you when at the first opportunity . . .'

'Nothing went on!' Sarah had been taking off her parka, unwinding her muffler, kicking off her boots, but she turned round to stare unbelievingly at the doctor. 'You can't believe that I spent three hours in that locker, in this appalling cold, making love!'

'Can I not?' His expression was grim. 'I've known Alan Wilde a little longer than you have, and, what's more, I saw you when I first opened that door, wrapped in his arms, so please don't play the innocent with me! Alan's a handsome fellow and very persuasive I don't doubt, but that's no reason to behave like . . . like that.'

'Alan put his arms round me because we were cold and it was dark and rather frightening in that locker. The only games we played were quizzes and I Spy! So please don't judge others by yourself!'

As soon as the words were out she regretted them, but she could not unsay them. Instead she continued to face him defiantly, her colour high.

'What do you mean by that?'

It was impossible, of course, to remind him what had happened in the shower without breaking his imposed ban on the subject, and anyway, she had no desire to refer to it. She decided to brazen it out.

'I mean just what I said! I assume that, had you been locked up in the dark with a woman, you would have taken advantage of the situation, since you accuse Alan. I think that's a fair judgment to make, in the circumstances.'

Dr Rothwell's mouth tightened.

'I can assure you, Nurse Barford, that you aren't irresistible, and neither am I as susceptible as Alan. I've known Alan for quite a while, and I know that he likes women, is popular with them, enjoys conquests. But this discussion is getting us nowhere. Just remember that I'll be watching you closely in future. I accept your explanation because I take your point about the cold and the dark, but if you do have an affair with any of the men I'll make sure you don't get a top job when we reach England again.'

Sarah waited a moment, simmering, but it seemed that he had finished his lecture. She turned and opened the door, half expecting to be called back, for she had said not a word of agreement or acknowledgement of having heard that last, outrageous remark. But he had moved behind the desk and appeared to be absorbed in some papers he was examining so she went out and shut the door crisply behind her.

In her own cabin, she examined her flushed and humiliated face in the mirror. How dare he say things like that to her, just on the flimsy evidence of having seen Alan's arms round her for a second or so? All that talk of giving her a bad report sounded very like blackmail and she was powerless to do anything, since whatever she might say a doctor's adverse report would be taken very seriously by anyone who might come across it.

Fuming, she began to change out of her jeans and sweater into a dress. For all her brave words, she did want at least the chance of a job on a cruise ship. Opportunities of unusual nursing jobs had never come her way, and she could well believe that Kurt Rothwell would see that they never did if she annoyed him. It was so unfair, when you thought how very badly he had behaved when she had been frozen and incapable of self-defence, yet she could never say anything about his behaviour without bringing her own into disrepute.

She had put on her cream silk jersey dress and

was winding a string of coral round her throat when it occurred to her that, had Dr Rothwell's remarks been made by anyone else, she would have assumed they were caused by jealousy. She raised her eyebrows at her reflection. Could it be jealousy? Oh, he would not want her, or not in any sense other than the most physical and basic, but he was so damned arrogant that he might well construe it as an insult if she appeared to prefer another man aboard to himself!

She began to knot her hair into a French pleat, then defiantly shook it out loose and brushed it vigorously into a mass of gleaming curls. For goodness' sake, why should she let anyone dictate what she wore or how she did her hair? Whatever she did was bound to be wrong so far as Dr Rothwell was concerned! She had spent a miserable afternoon shut in a cold and dirty locker with a man for whom she felt only the mildest friendship, and Dr Rothwell had accused her of carrying on with Alan, so no doubt he would find fault with her whether she looked her prettiest or her plainest. She would look as nice as she knew how, and let him do his worst!

'That's a cracking dress, Sarah. You look even prettier than you did in the locker.'

Sarah, sipping tinned tomato soup, smiled primly at Alan.

'Fie, sire, you flatter me! Especially when you remember that it was pitch dark in the locker, and that if I hadn't spoken every now and then, you wouldn't have known it if was me or the bo'sun!'

Don grinned and leaned curiously across the table.

'You mean that in three hours he didn't so much as . . .'

'No he didn't,' Sarah cut in quickly, hoping she was not blushing but very much fearing that she was. She had been prepared for ribbing, but not for the icy, watchful silence in which Kurt Rothwell sat, acting, she thought furiously, more like a circuit judge than a member of a team.

'What do you think, Kurt?' Don's tone was light. 'Are they telling the truth? It sounds incredible that Alan got our Sarah all to himself for three whole hours and spent it playing Twenty Questions!'

'Yes, incredible,' Dr Rothwell's tone was dry. 'However, I think we'll have to give them the benefit of the doubt. So long as it doesn't happen again.'

The others took it as a joke, seeming not to notice the underlying menace in the doctor's voice, but Sarah was not fooled. Nor, she thought, glancing round the table, was Stan. He was looking thoughtfully at Dr Rothwell, with a good deal of understanding in his glance.

'Perhaps we're all too fond of Sarah as a team member to want to make passes at her when she's at a disadvantage,' Stan suggested now. 'Anyhow, isn't it time we changed the subject? The poor girl's told you she was bored to tears with Alan's party games for three hours, and now you want to bore her all over again, teasing her about it.'

'It was only a joke,' Don said. 'You didn't mind, did you, Nursie?'

Sarah flashed Stan a grateful glance.

'Well, you do rather labour a joke and this one seems to have gone on forever. How about Alan coming clean and telling you about the plankton porridge?'

As she had guessed it would, this turned their attention to Alan, who had been looking a little peeved over her steady refusal to pretend that an amorous interlude had taken place. Now he grinned and pushed a lock of dark gold hair off his forehead.

'Oh, is *that* why she spurned my advances! Chaps, I had the appalling bad luck to be bearing in my arms at the time of our incarceration a net full of plankton porridge, and to tell the truth I tipped the lot all over myself, in my boots, down my duffel, probably even in my hair. I thought Sarah's voice went a trifle cold when I suggested cuddling up!' When the laughter died down, he added, 'Was that it, Sarah?'

'BO,' hissed Don, to more laughter. 'I must admit that if Princess Di herself approached me with plankton porridge in her hair, I'd spurn her advances!'

'At least I know it wasn't my lack of charm,' Alan said. 'Dear Sarah, I don't always smell like that.'

'You do,' Stan jibed. 'All marine biologists smell of plankton—didn't you know? That's how we can tell you even on the darkest night. It's true, isn't it, Sarah?'

'I shan't comment.' Sarah picked up her plate and headed for the hatch. 'Let's get dinner finished, and then I'm going to help Hughie make toffee.'

'Toffee? You're just a child at heart, Nurse Barford.' Stan collected the other plates and pushed them through the hatch to Hughie. 'Why not add a jar of peanut butter? When I was small my mother used to make the best peanut-butter toffee in the world, I've not tasted it for years.'

The other men, queueing at the hatch for their next course, were all occupied, their attention elsewhere. Sarah patted Stan's arm.

'You're a darling, Stan, to get me so neatly out of being teased. I'll make you some peanut-butter toffee as a reward!'

'How's it coming, eh, gal?' Hughie, sitting comfortably at his ease in the huge, creaking basket chair by the galley fire, peered curiously over to where Sarah stood by the stove. 'Been cookin' a while now, hasn't it?'

'I think it's nearly done,' Sarah said, lifting her spoon out of the bubbling, sweet-smelling mixture. 'Shove that pan of water nearer the edge of the table, will you, and I'll drop a spoonful in and see if it hardens.' She suited action to her words, then fished the toffee out and popped it into her mouth. 'Mmm, delicious,' she mumbled. 'Want to try it?'

'Aye, I wouldn't mind.' Hughie received a piece of warm toffee and chewed, then swallowed. 'That's real nice, gal! Where's your buttered tin, eh?'

'Here.' Sarah left the cooker and poured her mixture into the prepared tin. 'Another time, I'll make fudge; I love making it but it does go rather quickly.'

'So do I!' Alan, entering the galley unobserved by either of them, squeezed Sarah's waist appreciatively and nuzzled his cheek against her hair. 'Give us some, cooky!'

'Alan, leave off, you made me jump,' Sarah said

rather crossly, trying to pull away. 'You can't have any now until it cools, you know.'

'Scrape the saucepan and I'll have the bits on the spoon,' Alan said. 'I've come to help you wash up and then I'll take you on a tour of my cabin in the dark and prove that marine biologists smell deliciously masculine, of after-shave and tobacco, things like that.'

Sarah scraped the pan and handed him the spoon.

'I see. *Not* plankton.'

'That's right. And after proving I don't smell of plankton I'll show you my etchings. Or my samples of krill. Or the socks my mother knitted for me. Anything, I'll do anything!'

'Krill's only another name for plankton, you can't fool me,' Sarah scoffed, scoring across the tin of toffee with a knife. 'Thanks for the offer, but I find it possible to resist. In fact, easy. Dr Rothwell doesn't approve of assignations in cabins.'

'Rothwell? What does young love care for him? Oh come on, Sarah, be a sport! It's maddening never seeing you alone, all I want is a chat, so that I can tell you take me seriously.'

'I do take you seriously, as a marine biologist and fellow team member,' Sarah said, beginning to wash up her pans and spoons. 'But apart from that you just don't register, any more than anyone else does. I want to prove myself a capable and efficient nurse, you see, so I've no time for dalliance.'

'I don't even register?' Alan's voice was incredulous. 'Oh, come on, Sarah, you're only human for all your uniform! I'm a man and you're a woman, I must register with you!'

Hughie leaned forward and his basket chair creaked protestingly.

'Come on, boyo, that's a bit old-hat, the "I'm a man and you're a woman" bit, I mean. Sarah's here to do a job, same's the rest of us. Just you let her get on with it.'

Alan seized a heavy saucepan and began drying it vigorously.

'What a load of nonsense, Hughie. She did a job at the General, didn't she, and very well too, I daresay, but did that prevent her from having normal man-woman relationships off the ward? Of course it didn't! I can't bear this attitude that if you've got a career you aren't interested in anything else. If Sarah says that, she's just challenging me to prove her wrong.'

'Don't consider me a challenge or you'll end up getting me really cross, Alan,' Sarah said quickly. 'Anyway, this is all a bit sudden. Why should you decide out of the blue that you want to get to know me better? Just because we were shut in the locker together for three hours, and nothing happened?'

'Of course not! Well, perhaps, in a way. Of course I thought you were a damned pretty girl before then, but . . .'

'For God's sake!' Sarah turned from the sink and glared at him, her voice rising. 'I don't want to be rude, but haven't I made myself perfectly clear? I'm here to do a job and the last thing I want is what you call a man-woman relationship with anyone. *Anyone*, do you hear me? So just leave me alone, or I'll have to speak to Dr Rothwell.'

Alan glared back, then lunged clumsily across the galley and grabbed her, planting a badly-aimed kiss at the side of her mouth. His arms strained her to him despite Sarah desperately pushing against his chest.

'Rubbish, girl, don't be coy. Every woman wants . . .'

'I am *not* being coy!' Sarah, trembling with temper, dug her nails into his muscles and tried to scratch him, but his sweaters were too thick. 'Get away from me! Hughie, would you . . .'

'Certainly.' But while Hughie was still heaving himself ponderously out of his basket chair, Alan pushed her away so sharply that she cracked her hip painfully against the sink. He stormed out, slamming the door behind him so hard that the mugs on the hooks rattled and jumped.

'Well!' Sarah exclaimed. There were tears of annoyance in her eyes and she blinked furiously, refusing to let them fall. 'Of all the conceited, self-opinionated . . .'

'He ain't so bad.' Hughie patted her shoulder clumsily. 'He's young and you hurt his pride; see?'

'Yes, but what am I supposed to do?' Sarah wailed. 'Fall into his arms when that's the last place I want to be? I've got my pride too, you know.'

'Well now, I should think . . .' Hughie was beginning, when the galley door opened. Dr Rothwell stood there.

'Could you spare me a moment, Sarah?'

Sarah sighed very, very softly, put down the pan she was drying and turned away from the sink. Her boss looked a trifle grim.

'Of course, sir.' She was gratified to see that a soft answer, in this instance at any rate, had turned away wrath, for Dr Rothwell looked almost mollified. 'In the office, sir?'

'Yes. Finish that drying up. Shall we say in five minutes?'

'I'll be there, sir.' He left the galley and Sarah turned to Hughie, despair in her face. 'Now what, do you suppose? Dr Rothwell thinks I encouraged Alan, you know. He's been quite nasty about us being shut in the locker already, and if Alan's going to make a dead set at me I don't think I can stand it. And did you notice how smarmy I was, all that bowing and scraping and tugging my forelock? It doesn't come naturally to me to be so polite to a man like Kurt Rothwell.'

'I did notice you said "sir" every other word,' Hughie admitted, grinning. 'Do you good, girl, teach you respect for your elders! As for Alan, you'll just have to keep him at arm's length, and then the doc will see you mean well.'

'It's no use, wrathful Rothwell believes I'm a wicked woman who lures men into her cabin to chase seagulls, and shuts them up in chain lockers,' Sarah groaned. 'Oh, Hughie, why is my life so complicated?'

Hughie laughed and began to put the pans away.

'I've heard it said, gal, that they didn't intend to have a female aboard, and that when the doc tried to send you ashore you threatened him with the Equal Opportunities board. I daresay he's set on making you see he was right all along.'

'Ye-es. It makes me almost wish I hadn't . . . No, I don't, I'm *glad* I stood up to Dr Rothwell and forced him to let me stay. And I'll *prove* I can cope. I'll keep Alan at arm's length and do my job and get all the fun I can out of it, what's more.'

'Good for you, that's the spirit!' Hughie encouraged. 'And now go and tell the doc how you feel. Stand up to him, gal. He's one that admires spirit.'

'Not in me he doesn't,' Sarah said gloomily, leaving the galley. 'He wants his nurses meek and biddable.'

Hughie's chuckle followed her down the corridor.

'Ah, Nurse. Sit down a moment, please.'

Dr Rothwell, sitting behind his desk, gestured Sarah to the chair before it. 'Now! Would you please tell me why you wore an extremely . . . a very clinging dress for dinner tonight, and left your hair loose, after my warning?'

Sarah, who had changed into jeans and a sweater as soon as the meal finished, glanced down at herself as if she expected the dress to magically reappear.

'Dress?' She saw his mouth tighten ominously and decided to try total frankness. 'Oh, the white dress! I wore it to cheer myself up and give myself courage. I didn't enjoy being shut up in that locker despite what you may have thought, and so I thought I'd make the best of myself for once. Why?'

'Because it looked as though you were dressing up for Alan. I'm sure that was how he interpreted it.'

Sarah sighed.

'I don't agree but if you're right, I've disillusioned him. In fact, he probably hates me. Is that all, sir?'

He was shuffling through some papers trying to find something and now he glanced up at her. Her heart gave a painful lurch. He was so handsome when he was pleased with her, when the blue of his eyes was softened.

'Well, almost. The rest is strictly business. I want you to do urinalysis tests tomorrow morning, on everyone aboard. Everything's ready, so if you could hand out containers tonight and get the men to bring them along to the sickbay first thing tomorrow, you can spend the morning checking them for blood and glucose. All right?'

'Yes, I suppose . . .' Sarah found that though she had no objection to requesting urine samples from patients in hospital, it would not be so easy to ask for them from the men with whom she worked. But Dr Rothwell was watching her, waiting for her to say she could not do it.

'Very well, sir.' She got up and went over to where the urine flasks stood. With her back to him, she said: 'Did you take a bottle for yourself, sir?'

'Yes. Tell the men an early, midstream sample.'

Sarah nodded and left the room. He was being difficult on purpose, she had no doubt of that! It was tempting to wander back in and suggest that he might take the containers round to the team and the crew, but that was doubtless what he was expecting her to do. No, she would not give him the satisfaction of admitting that she felt rather foolish asking men she knew well to fill the bottles for her. She would blush unseen!

CHAPTER SIX

HANDING out the small flasks, neatly labelled, with a napkin over each, proved, in the end, to be much easier than she had anticipated. Sarah simply put on her uniform and her most forbidding expression and took the containers round just as the men were about to go off to bed. The team, scientists to a man, received her offering with various rude and wry comments and disappeared into their cabins, but the crew were slightly more obtuse, one engineer even going so far as to ask her with what she wanted the flask filled?

'With a urine sample,' Sarah said crisply, suppressing a desire to reply, in song "With water, dear Liza, dear Liza, dear Liza," and made her escape whilst the engineer, a short, thickset man named Connelly, was asking his mates, in a broad Scots accent, 'Wha' the lassie might mean, noo'.

Finally, she checked the list of names against the ship's complement and made her way to bed, reflecting that she had done her best and few could say more.

At nine o'clock the next morning, standing in the sickbay counting the filled flasks, she felt she had done rather well. Preparation beforehand is the thing, she thought smugly, moving across to the counter where her results' sheet, typed up and only needing the details filled in, awaited her. This job would take scarcely any time now.

Dr Rothwell came in and glanced across at her. He was clad in duffel and boots, obviously ready for a trip on deck.

'Everything going according to plan, Sarah?'

Since I'm Sarah again, he must be in a better mood, Sarah thought optimistically, but aloud she just said politely: 'Yes thank you, sir,' and continued to line up her samples.

She was disturbed only twice in the course of her analysis, once to dispense some cough medicine to Albert, who complained that his cough was waking him up during the night, and once to lance a painful looking boil on the back of the chief engineer's neck.

Despite her hopes, however, all was not to be totally straightforward. She tested the last sample, pencilled in the result and moved away from the surface to put the empty bottles into the steriliser when it struck her that one column was still empty. She glanced at it. Oh, no! It looked as though Alan Wilde had not handed in a sample.

She stood frowning down at the list for a moment, sorely tempted. Of all the people she knew, the men aboard the *Ice Venture* were the fittest; without a shadow of a doubt she would hunt for Alan, demand his sample, test it, and find he was as healthy as all the others. Bli stick after Bli stick she had inserted in the bottles, with her fob watch laid on the counter to count the seconds. Bli stick after Bli stick had shown yellow for a negative blood content and light turquoise for negative sugar content. She was sure Alan's sample would be no different—suppose she just filled in his column the same as all the others and forgot to chase him up?

But it would never do. Her training forbade it, and besides, if there was something wrong with Alan . . . she shuddered at what Dr Rothwell would say to her. Alan knew quite well that he was supposed to hand in a sample at nine this morning. He might be withholding it just because, as a scientist, he knew something *was* wrong.

However, conjecture would get her nowhere. Sarah put the empty bottles into the steriliser, turned it on to full, and tidied up. Then she reached for her muffler and parka. She had better go and check that Alan was not on deck, then she could check all the other places on the ship where he might be. She would ask him to bring the sample down right away or, if by some mischance it was still in his cabin, she would offer to fetch it for him.

In the event, she did not have to go on deck. Meeting Don in the corridor, he told her that Alan had been working most of the night and had decided to get a few hours' sleep before lunch.

'Working all night? Why ever did he do that?'

'Oh, he and Fred got a bright idea for keeping the whaleback clear of ice. It involved the use of rather a lot of electrical wiring and meant that first the whaleback had to be cleared of the ice already on it. Since night is no darker than day now, Alan and Fred got two of the crew who were off watch to help them, and they chunked the ice off the whaleback and then laid their wires. It seems to be working, too. It's still clear this morning, though a lot more ice has built up elsewhere overnight.'

'I see. Well, I want a word with Alan. Do you think he'll still be sleeping?'

Don shrugged.

'Dunno. What's the time?'

Sarah consulted her wristwatch. 'Noon.'

'He'll be getting up soon, I should think, Alan's never been known to miss a meal! Why not speak to him at lunchtime?'

But Sarah had no desire for a lunchtime confrontation over the missing urine sample.

'No, I'd rather speak to him now. I'll knock on his door and wake him, I think—after all, lunch is in forty minutes. Thanks, Don.'

Her knock was greeted with a cheerful bellow of 'What's up now?' so Sarah opened the door a crack and spoke through it.

'Alan? Are you decent? It's me, Sarah.'

'Come in, Sal. I fell into bed at about 5 a.m. and slept like a log until five minutes ago. What can I do for you?'

Sarah, her question as to Alan's decency unanswered, remained in the corridor. She had no desire to walk into his cabin and find him cheerfully naked at the handbasin.

'It's the sample, Alan. Yours wasn't handed in, so I thought I'd better remind you.'

There was a rustle, then the sound of feet padding across the floor, and Alan appeared in the doorway, looking self-conscious. He was clad in a pair of jeans and a t-shirt, and clapped a hand to his head at her words.

'Oh damn, I clean forgot! Look, give me five minutes and I'll bring it down to sickbay. I've got to get dressed for lunch, anyway. Will that be all right?'

'Yes, that'll be fine,' Sarah said, preparing to

depart. 'It's just a formality, of course, but it has to
be done.'

'Right. I'll be with you in five minutes.'

Sarah returned to the sickbay to find, in her
absence, that Dr Rothwell had plonked a pile of his
scribbled notes by her typewriter. Sighing, she
glanced at it to see whether she should start on the
work at once, or leave it until she had eaten. None
of it was marked urgent, however, so she stacked
the papers beside her machine again and went over
to the bench to lay out her testing equipment once
more.

As good as his word, Alan walked in five minutes
later, the full sample bottle in one hand.

'There we are, Nurse B! Can I sit next to you at
lunch?'

'I just want to do the tests on this,' Sarah said.
'You go on, Alan, and I'll catch you up.'

But at that moment, Dr Rothwell put his head
round the door.

'Sarah, I want . . . Oh, it's you, Wilde.'

There could be no mistaking the animosity in his
tone.

'That's right, Kurt, little old me. Do you object?'

There was no mistaking the challenge in Alan's
voice, either. Sarah looked apprehensively from
one man to the other. Surely they were not going to
start another argument?

But she had reckoned without her boss's un-
doubted urbanity.

'Not in the least. However, I wanted to see
Sarah's results and talk to her about my notes and
when I saw you, I realised that it's lunchtime. Are
you coming along to the mess deck?'

Sarah had donned rubber gloves and apron again, but now she stripped off the gloves, slipped out of the apron, and unpinned her cap. She rarely wore uniform at lunchtime since the afternoons were usually given over to deckwork and helping in the galley but usually she had a chance to change before lunch. Today was obviously going to be different.

'I'll go up as I am today, then. I've only one more sample to test and I can do that after I've eaten, before I go up on deck.'

'You won't be going up on deck this afternoon. I've a lot of notes waiting to be typed out.'

Sarah bristled at the command in her boss's tone. Why could he never *ask*?

'Oh? Who'll do Stan's work, then?'

'Me.'

The monosyllable was not conducive to discussion and nothing further was said until they reached the mess deck, when the talk became general.

It was a good lunch, and Sarah ate with a will and allowed the usual steady stream of banter and exclamation to flow over her head. Dr Rothwell, too, was quieter than usual and Alan, who had managed to sit next to Sarah, scarcely opened his mouth except to put food into it.

'You're a cook in a million, Hughie,' Sarah remarked as she handed her empty pudding plate through the hatch at the conclusion of the meal. 'I'm sorry I can't give you a hand with the washing up, but I've nearly finished the urinalysis, so I'm going straight back to the sickbay to clear up and get my results typed.'

'That's all right, love, I'll shanghai someone else

into giving a hand,' Hughie assured her. 'You do more than your share, I reckon.'

Back in the sickbay, Sarah donned apron and gloves once more and reached for the remaining sample. She lay down her fob watch, inserted her Bli stick, noted the negative reaction for blood and then glanced at the indicator for glucose, her mind already writing 'normal' neatly on the sheet and putting it aside.

Except that it was not. If there had been no glucose in the sample the stick would have shown turquoise, a trace of glucose would have given it a speckled brown appearance. Only in the presence of considerable glucose should it be dark brown all over.

It was dark brown all over. Sarah stared, then laid the Bli stick down on a dish and reached for another, knowing that there was a chance in a million that the first stick had been faulty, yet unable to believe the evidence of her own eyes. Alan a diabetic! It seemed impossible, it certainly said nothing of the sort in his notes, yet it was not unheard of for someone to become a diabetic overnight, she supposed. Only Alan seemed so fit, so healthy.

The second test, done with a wildly thumping heart, was exactly the same as the first. Sarah entered her finding on the record sheet, carefully resealed the sample bottle, and slowly stripped off her rubber gloves. She must find Dr Rothwell and see what he had to say about this. It could not be her fault, exactly, yet it did seem strange . . .

She put on her outer clothing and made for the deck. This, she felt, constituted an emergency, and the doctor had made it plain that she should always consult him in an emergency.

When she reached the deck they were clearing ice. It was building up faster than even the steam hoses could clear it, and though some of the new chemicals were very efficient, their efficiency did not seem to last very long. They could get the ice clear, but unless one was prepared to stand on the deck and use the chemical sprays twenty-four hours a day, the ice built up again with an inexorability which was frightening.

Walking carefully, she approached Dr Rothwell, who was clearing the scuppers the old-fashioned way—with an axe. He was laying about him with a will, and when he saw her and turned towards her she saw that sweat beaded his forehead despite the cold and that his chest was rising and falling rapidly with his exertions.

'Yes?'

'I wonder if you'd mind coming down to the sickbay for a moment, Doctor? Something's arisen which I think you ought to see. You did say . . .'

He was always decisive, and now was no exception. No questions, no dithering. He just put down his axe and crossed the deck at her side, diving down the companionway behind her and overtaking her in the corridor to reach the door of the sickbay first and fling it open, ushering her within.

'Well?' He unwound his muffler and began to take off his duffelcoat, his keen eyes scanning her face. 'What is it?'

Sarah took off her own coat and mittens, then walked over to the work bench. She picked up the last Bli stick and held it out.

'My last test, sir. It's very positive.'

He took it from her fingers.

'Hmm. That's bad. Whose is it?'

She wished she could say any name but Alan's, because the last thing she wanted to do was to keep bringing the poor fellow to Dr Rothwell's attention, but there was no alternative.

'Alan Wilde, sir.'

'Hmm. Have you told him?'

'No.' Sighing, she indicated the record sheet. 'I kept thinking I must have made a mistake, that's why I tested it twice, but there was no doubt of the result either time.'

He ran his finger down the record sheet. He was frowning.

'Wilde's is the last name, I see. Just a coincidence, or was there some other reason?'

'No, Alan was working all night and forgot to bring his sample up this morning. I had to chase him for it at lunchtime.'

Dr Rothwell's brow cleared.

'I see! He gave you the bottle after lunch, then?'

'No. Before.'

'Oh. That's not the answer, then. Unless . . .' he moved towards the door. 'Stay here. I'll have a word with Wilde.'

He was gone a bare five minutes. When he re-entered the room he was grinning. He walked over to the record sheet and drew a thick black line through the last entry, then he turned to her, his smile gone, his expression stern.

'It's a great relief to know it was a mistake but really, Nurse, you must be more careful! You went to Wilde's cabin to fetch the sample—did it not

occur to you when he told you he'd bring it down in
five minutes that he had, in fact, forgotten to fill the
bottle this morning?'

Sarah felt a blush creep across her cheeks. So he
had forgotten to fill the bottle! But even so . . .

'It did occur to me, sir, but I knew he had had no
breakfast and there was another half hour before
lunch, so it seemed to me that it was still probably
his "early" sample.'

'It simply never occurred to you to ask Wilde if
he'd eaten recently?'

Poor Sarah's cheeks were burning.

'Oh heavens, don't tell me that rustling sound I
heard . . .'

He was nodding, his expression mocking.

'That's right. A half pound slab of milk chocolate! No wonder you got a positive reading!'

Relief and guilt combined to make her quite
lightheaded.

'Of course!' She collapsed against the desk and
began to giggle. 'What a fool I was! I never thought
of chocolate, I just thought that he'd forgotten to
bring the sample down, or that he was giving me an
"early" anyway! Panic over, then.'

Dr Rothwell came across to the desk. His eyebrows were almost meeting and the expression in
his blue eyes was cold.

'Panic, Nurse Barford, ought to be about to
begin, for you, at any rate. How could you be so
silly, after I've warned you? "I didn't think" will be
carved on your tombstone, I should imagine. Do
you realise that if I'd not had a shrewd suspicion
that Wilde had probably eaten sweets just before
providing the sample, you might have started a real

panic? It's carelessnesses like these which will make people fight shy of employing you in the meanest capacity.'

Sarah tightened her lips.

'Dr Rothwell, you aren't being very fair. Alan's a scientist, a man of some intelligence. He was told last night, loud and clear, that I wanted an early sample, that the bottle must be filled before he had so much as sipped a cup of tea. Is it expecting too much to assume that he would have remembered such explicit instructions? And what's more, I had no idea that anyone kept food in their cabins. You must have known that Alan liked sweet things in between meals—you said you knew him better than I did!'

She glared up at him and to her surprise he actually smiled, looking a good deal more human.

'Prior knowledge, in fact, saved me from falling into error. You're right, as it happens. When I looked at the lab stick my first reaction was that of all the men aboard, Alan was the one most likely to become diabetic, because of all the chocolate and sweets he's perpetually eating.' He glanced at her, a brow rising quizzically. 'Didn't he produce anything edible from his pockets during your incarceration?'

'Not a thing, though now that you mention it, I remember that he keeps a tube of mints in his duffel as a rule, and hands them round before we go out on deck.'

'There, you see, you can be quite observant! In future, never forget that scientists are not only human but notoriously absent-minded about anything unconnected with their own work. Instructions given by a slip of a girl can easily be forgotten or ignored when minds are worrying over a problem which seems to a scientist to be much more important. Check and double check in future, Sarah.'

'Yes, sir.' Sarah slid off the desk and went round to sit in front of her typewriter. 'Shall I get on with typing up your notes, now?'

'All right. I've told Wilde to provide you with another sample first thing tomorrow morning, so you can do your tests on that. By the way, I see in the treatment book that you lanced a boil on Chiefie's neck. You didn't use a local? No complications?'

'No, it was straightforward. The boil was ripe, the blade barely touched it to be honest, but Chiefie was full of praise for what he called my painless operation!'

'I see. What dressing was it that you used?'

She glanced up at him defensively. Was he testing her in some way?

'It's all in the treatment book, sir, and if you want to take a look at my handiwork come to clinic tomorrow morning. Chiefie's coming in daily for dressings.'

He turned and made for the door, then stopped with it half open.

'Thank you, Nurse, but I'll take your word—and the treatment book's—that the job's been done properly,' there was a pause, 'This time.'

'That,' Sarah said, crimsoning with justifiable rage, 'Was the most unfair . . .'

But she was speaking to a closed door.

*

Had she been given a choice, Sarah would have much preferred to keep the affair of the secret chocolate eater, as she termed it, to herself. But Alan, it seemed, had no such inhibitions. He made a good story out of how his secret vice had very nearly led to the ending of diplomatic relations between nurse and doctor, and how he himself had suffered a great dressing-down at Kurt's hands. Sarah consequently came in for a good deal of ribbing on the subject of samples various and this one in particular, and could only be grateful when a worsening of the weather took the minds of the team off such trivialities.

'Imagine hauling a trawl net in that,' Alan gasped one day, meeting Sarah at the foot of the companionway as he staggered down from a session on deck. 'It's hell out there, Sarah! The ice has covered everything, and the Captain's got the wind up in case the radar mast freezes up, so the crew seem to spend most of their time trying to keep it mobile. And have you seen the growlers? Mini-icebergs everywhere, to say nothing of visibility down to zero because of heavy seas, and fog, or simply because the snow's blowing a blizzard. You're not going up there?'

'I am. I'm being Stan's strong right arm, since the doctor decided that he can't keep a good man down a moment longer. I think Stan must have threatened him with the Equal Opportunities Board, judging from Dr Rothwell's expression when he came out of his office!'

'Rothwell's got no right to ask it of you,' Alan muttered. 'The wind's strong enough to blow you right across the deck.' He put his hands on her shoulders and peered down into her face. 'Want me to come along as anchor man? I don't mind, you know.'

'Thanks, Alan, but you look worn out already,' Sarah said. 'We'll be okay, Stan's pretty strong.'

'You're well wrapped up, I hope? Two pairs of socks?'

Sarah heaved an exaggerated sigh and tried to wriggle out from beneath Alan's hands.

'Yes, Nanny! I've got three sweaters on, and my parka's buttoned and zipped, I know to pull the muffler over my face the instant the door opens, I've got double socks on, both pairs pure wool, and my mittens are fur-lined, and . . .'

'Damn it, Sal, I want to make sure you're not going to get into trouble,' Alan said in an aggrieved voice. 'You know how I feel about you, I didn't intend to make a fool of myself by falling for you, but . . . hang it, you don't give a fellow a chance to show . . .'

He lunged at her, and they were struggling in each other's arms, with Sarah trying to free herself and Alan trying to kiss her, when the door of the mess deck opened and Stan came out, closely followed by Dr Rothwell. Both men stopped short. 'Nurse!'

The harsh note in Dr Rothwell's voice at least had the effect of bringing Alan back to the present. He moved back, colour rising to his cheeks, his hands loosening their grip on Sarah's arms, and Sarah took advantage of his surprise to move quickly up the corridor towards the two men.

'Yes, sir? I was coming to help Stan, but Alan

thought . . . he's been up on deck and he . . . we . . .'

'It isn't necessary to explain away your behaviour, Nurse.' Dr Rothwell's voice was cutting. 'Since the weather is severe, I'm going to keep a firm grip on Stan whilst you check the instruments. When the wind's not so bad, we'll probably let you do some of your own work,' he added, in a kinder tone, to Stan.

'I'm being a damned nuisance, I know,' Stan said, as they climbed the companionway. 'But I felt I *had* to get out, take a look at the readings for myself, instead of being stuck below deck day in, day out.'

'Well, I'll try to get you up on deck now, once a day at least,' Dr Rothwell said, pulling up his muffler and pushing the steel door ajar. 'Take care!' The wind hurled itself at the door, and it took the doctor's whole strength to force it open for long enough for the three of them to emerge on deck. 'Glory! Watch yourselves!'

They fought their way across the deck, and Sarah realised that Alan had not been exaggerating. It was all she could do to keep her feet, and with the snow and hail whipping against her face and the strength of the wind, she could hope to make very little progress. But she was determined not to hang onto either of the men—they had their own battle to fight with Stan's plastered arm and, anyway, she still hated Dr Rothwell for so obviously misinterpreting her struggle with Alan Wilde in the corridor just now.

They reached the partial shelter of the whaleback at last, and Dr Rothwell gestured to her to take readings whilst he kept Stan braced against the weather. Sarah moved forward, bent to peer at the instrument nearest her—and then something cannoned violently against her and she found herself sprawling on the deck with what felt like a good-sized elephant sitting in the small of her back.

'What on earth . . . ? Ouch!' The exclamation came as she tried to struggle upright and felt a sudden, sharp pain stab at her ribs. Then she was hauled to her feet by Dr Rothwell whilst Stan, bent double, took the readings himself. The doctor put his mouth close to her ear.

'Can you walk? That was a bad fall.'

Sarah nodded shakily, unwilling to admit that she had been hurt though she ached all over.

'Good. Stan!'

Stan could not have heard but at that moment he finished taking his readings and stood up, gesturing back towards the companionway. Even Stan, so eager to be out, must have realised that nothing more could be achieved whilst the storm continued.

Once safe and sheltered in the corridor at the bottom of the companionway, the three of them pushed back their hoods, pulled down their mufflers, and gazed ruefully at each other.

'That must be the worst gale I've ever tried to work in,' Stan observed. 'What happened to you two? One moment Sarah was bending over to get the readings, the next Kurt was sitting in the middle of her back, with our poor girl flat on her face on deck!'

'Oh, so it was you!' Sarah turned a steely eye on her boss. 'You're overweight, Dr Rothwell, I thought the funnel had fallen on me!'

'I slipped,' Dr Rothwell said briefly. 'Fortunately I landed more or less on top of you, and you're well padded with all that clothing so neither of us were hurt.'

'Fortunately?' Sarah took a deep breath to tell the doctor what she thought of him and a pain stabbed viciously through her rib cage. 'I'm not a cushion, you know,' she concluded, quite mildly.

'Sorry, just an expression.' Dr Rothwell took her arm. 'I daresay I landed hard, though, so I'd better just check you over.'

Once in the sickbay, Sarah shrugged herself out of her coat and bent to take off her boots. She could not prevent a tiny gasp of pain as she did so, but hoped that Dr Rothwell, taking off his own outdoor things, would have noticed nothing. As soon as he was free of his coat and boots, he turned to her.

'Over here, please, Sarah. Stretch your arms out straight in front of you.'

'There's no *need*, sir, I'm fine, just a bit bruised.'

'I'm glad to hear it. Do as you're told, please.'

Sarah, seeing defeat approaching at a gallop, surrendered with an ill grace and stretched out her arms.

'I fell a bit heavily, that's all,' she said sulkily. 'I may have fractured a rib and if I have there's nothing you can do about it, so why worry? Anyhow, I'm sure I haven't fractured a rib because it doesn't hurt enough, it's just a bit sharp when I breathe in deeply or when I lift my diaphragm or use my left arm.'

'I thought you squeaked just now,' Dr Rothwell said. 'Is the pain high or low?'

'It's one of the short ribs, on my left side,' Sarah

admitted grudgingly. 'But honestly, it scarcely hurts at all, and . . . ouch!'

'Hands on your hips, and don't wriggle,' Dr Rothwell ordered, having whipped up her blue sweater without so much as a by-your-leave. 'That's better.' His hands were gentle but firm on her rib cage, finding the tender spot, moving along to test the injured rib for further damage. At last, his examination over, he pulled her sweater down and patted her cheek.

'Cracked rib, just a haircrack I daresay, but you'll feel it sharp for a day or two. No point in doing anything about it, except to see that you do no deckwork for three days and rest as much as possible. No typing either, of course.'

'No deckwork? No typing? I'll die of boredom,' Sarah protested. 'What about the clinic? I've got to do that.'

'You can do the clinic,' Dr Rothwell conceded. 'The bruising will start to show soon and from tomorrow it'll start to knit.' He glanced at his wristwatch. 'There's an hour before tea, go and lie down and get some rest.' He turned away as if to go into the inner office, then turned back. 'There's one other activity that's not allowed, of course.'

'Oh, really? No eating, I suppose?'

'You can eat as much as you wish.' His glance was saturnine. 'But there must be no lovemaking, Nurse. It's very hard on the ribs, lovemaking. Will you tell Alan or shall I?'

Sarah flung herself out of the sickbay, slamming the door so loudly that even above the storm it seemed to echo in her ears as she hurried to her own cabin. That detestable man! No lovemaking, in-

deed! As if she had ever allowed Alan Wilde—or
anyone else—to make love to her. He was determined to see her in a bad light, that was the trouble.

She stalked over to the mirror and pulled up her
sweater. Faintly, a pattern of bruising was beginning to show up already. Sighing, she pulled the
sweaters off one by one, then sat down with a
thump on her bunk. What a thing to happen, and
how bored she was going to be doing nothing! And
the worst and most maddening thing was that
though it was undoubtedly Dr Rothwell's fault,
though he had sat in the middle of her back and
cracked her rib with his sheer weight and size, she
was sure that he would contrive to put all the blame
on her, in the end.

CHAPTER SEVEN

'GOOD morning, Mr Rogers. How's the neck?'

Sarah got up from behind her desk and moved across the cabin to where her first patient stood. Three days had passed and her rib scarcely hurt at all. She had every intention of typing today, though she supposed she had best pay lip service to authority and get Dr Rothwell's permission first. No point in antagonising him, since the partial truce which had been in force ever since she had cracked her rib had made life pleasanter.

'Much better thanks, Nurse. But you said to come back.'

'That's right. I like to take a look at my handiwork.' Sarah peeled the dressing off, to reveal the puckered scar from the enormous boil now looking pink and healthy. She touched it lightly, pressing it, searching for any build-up of pus beneath the healing skin, but there was none and it was cool to the touch. 'It's fine, Mr Rogers, couldn't be better. I'll put another dry dressing on, because it's so dirty in the engine room, but you needn't come back again.'

'That's good news. And how's your trouble?'

Not even a cracked rib went unnoticed on a ship the size of the *Ice Venture*, Sarah knew that. It was a tiny hotbed of gossip, where everyone's business was of the greatest interest to everyone else and though nothing had been said to her face, she knew that the relationship between herself and the doctor, and herself and Alan Wilde was watched with the keenest interest by every man aboard. Some were envious, some avuncular, some thought it a huge joke, but into whichever category they fell, they all wanted to know what went on and who was in favour.

'Do you mean my cracked rib? It's much better, thanks. I'm going to ask the doctor if I can start typing again today. His work's mounting up and I don't want to find myself snowed under so that I can't do any deckwork.'

'Enjoy deckwork, do you, Miss?'

'Yes, I do. It varies the monotony, and it's nice to breathe fresh air now and then, even through mufflers!'

As Rogers left the cabin one of the other team members, Albert Leman, walked in. He was a marine biologist, like Alan, and the two men were friends. He smiled at her and held out a hand, the palm of which was scored with what looked like a deep burn.

'Sorry, Sarah, I've done it again. Got any spare burn dressings?'

Sarah, wheeling her trolley into position and indicating that Albert should sit down, sighed.

'Oh, Albert, that's your third rope burn in a fortnight! You really should keep your mittens on, like the rest of us.' She examined his hand. 'It's quite deep this time, and the other's scarcely healed. How did you do it? Hauling the drift net in again?'

'Yes. Hand went numb, didn't realise, and the

rope slid through my grasp too fast.' He laughed, looking up at her. 'Story of my life! How are the ribs?'

'It's only one rib, and that's very well, thank you. I'm hoping to start some deckwork tomorrow.'

She had cleaned the wound, now she spread it lightly with ointment and then applied the dressing.

'That's excellent news.' Albert's eyes were on her face. 'Alan will be pleased!'

Sarah stiffened. 'I hope everyone will be pleased.' She bandaged the dressing firmly in place, then stood back. 'Keep those mittens on in future, please, Albert. It makes a lot of work for the other men when they have to take on your work too, because you've got rope burns.'

'I'll be good. Thanks, Sarah.' Albert stood up. 'You sounded rather severe just now. I'd have expected you to be singing and dancing at the thought of being back to normal.'

'What exactly do you mean by that?' Sarah pushed her trolley briskly back into its clips on the bulkhead. 'I trust there has been nothing abnormal about me since I cracked my rib.'

'Oh, well, you know.' Albert looked vaguely discomfited. 'I bet poor Alan wasn't allowed to give you the tiniest squeeze!'

'Alan isn't allowed to squeeze me anyway,' Sarah said coolly, sitting down at her desk. 'Believe it or not, I don't want his squeezes even when my ribs are in the pink of condition.'

'No?' Albert's smile was frankly sceptical. 'Alan's got quite a reputation, you know, for . . .'

'So have I!' Sarah stood up. 'I don't like people gossiping about me, when there's nothing to gossip about. I'm sick and tired of you chaps trying to link my name with Alan Wilde's.'

Dr Rothwell, entering at that point, raised a brow at her as the door shut behind a chastened Albert.

'Really? Well, that's good news. How does the rib feel?'

'Perfectly all right, thanks,' Sarah said promptly. 'I'd like to start work right away, sir, if you'll allow me.'

'Bruising gone?'

'Well, no, but it doesn't hurt, honestly.' She gazed earnestly up at him, determined to win her freedom from the restrictions imposed by the cracked rib. 'And if I don't start typing soon, I'll be completely swamped by your notes for the rest of the voyage.'

'It doesn't hurt to move, or to touch?'

'No, not at all.' She demonstrated by moving her arms vigorously, then patting her ribcage. 'See?'

He leaned across and coolly lifted her sweaters, eyed the bruising for a moment, then applied gentle pressure to the injury. Then he pulled her sweaters into position again and smiled.

'Either you're an extraordinarily stoical girl or you're telling the truth, and I'm inclined to believe it's the latter. Very well, on with the typing, but we won't talk about deckwork just yet. Conditions are pretty vile out there.'

'Thank you, sir.' Sarah sat down in her chair, threaded paper round the roller, and began to type.

It was later that same day that they lost power. Sarah was on the mess deck, helping Hughie out after lunch by clearing the tables, for the team had eaten hurriedly and gone rushing out again, when the lights went out. It was completely dark, the darkness of caves or cellars, and Sarah instinctively stayed absolutely still, waiting for light to be restored. She could hear, through the hatch, Hughie swear sharply, and then a crash as he bumped into something. Because there was silence from the engines, the sound of the stormy seas seemed louder and more menacing, and she was immensely relieved when Hughie's voice spoke to her through the thick dark.

'Sarah? You all right, gal?'

'I think so. But what happened? Are we sinking?'

'Sinking? No such thing!' Hughie's voice was matter of fact, tinged with amusement. It gave Sarah's confidence a considerable boost. 'Just an electrical fault, it'll be. I'll get us some light; can you make your way over to the hatch?'

Sarah's groping hands found the edge of the table. If she followed the edge along, it would lead her almost to the hatch.

Before she had progressed more than a foot, however, light returned. Not the brilliance of the ship's electricity, but the dim glow of a candle. Through the hatch, Hughie's beaming face, illumined from below, came into view. He held a candle in each hand.

'Here, gal, take one of these.' He pushed one of the candles through to her and she saw that it was wedged into a mug so that it would not easily be extinguished. 'Take it along to the bridge, make sure everyone's got a light of some sort, though the fellers mostly have torches. No one's on deck, I shouldn't think.'

Sarah, halfway to the door, stopped short, a hand flying to her mouth.

'Oh, my God!'

She did not wait for Hughie's questions, or for her own doubts to wake, she just headed for the companionway. During dinner, Dr Rothwell had made a joking remark about the trawling tackle, said that if all the scientists were too busy with their experiments in the fishroom which they were using, he would be forced to mount a one-man expedition onto the deck to chop the tackle free from ice. It had seemed like a joke—but supposing it had not been, suppose he had been serious?

Two minutes before, she would have sworn that nothing would have persuaded her to go onto the deck with only a candle in a mug for illumination. Now, she rushed into the galley and grabbed her parka, stuffing her arms into it as she ran along the corridor, thanking her stars that she was still wearing her sea-boots and that her muffler and mittens were in the capacious pockets of the coat.

She reached the foot of the companionway, then hesitated. Should she rush quickly along to the fishroom and make sure that Dr Rothwell was not there, working with the other team members? Or, if he was not, she would be on the spot to get all the help she might need. But she dared not lose a moment. He had been on the deck without lights for several moments, if he was indeed out there. To turn in the wrong direction in the dark, to miss the door with a big sea running—and there was always a big sea running now—could mean instant, icy death. Not drowning. Men did not drown in seas as cold as these. They were dead before they touched the water, Hughie had told her so many times.

She reached the steel door, flung it open and burst onto the deck. Snow whirled into her face but did not douse the candle for she was sheltering the top of the mug with one hand. She stared into the darkness.

At first, she could see nothing. Only the dark and the snow. And then, as her eyes grew accustomed to the night, she saw that there was light out there, that the sea itself, with the angry white-topped combers which were on a level with the deck, sometimes above it, glowed with some sort of phosphorescence, so that it was possible to look around the deck and pick out the whaleback, the lockers, the trawl and its tackle.

Then she saw him. It could, of course, have been anyone, for the figure sprawled on the ice was muffled beyond recognition, but she knew that it was Kurt Rothwell. He was lying on his back in the partial shelter of the trawl equipment, one arm thrown out, his head hard up against the super-structure.

She crossed the deck faster than she would have thought possible and bent over the inert figure. She touched his cheek, tore off her mitten with a sharp exclamation, and touched his cheek again.

It was cold. Was he dead? Her heart moved in her breast, the pain in it so acute that she gasped, and even as she moved back to fetch her candle in its mug for a closer examination, for she had put it down the moment she spotted the doctor, he moved.

'Doctor? Dr Rothwell!'

But that movement, it seemed, did not mean that he was regaining consciousness. He made no sign that he had heard her, and when she bent over him, trying to lift him, he sagged in her arms, far too heavy for her to move. However, with her arms tightly round him and her face against his, she felt, heartwarmingly, his breath on her cheek. He was alive then, albeit only just.

'Dr Rothwell, do wake up!'

She tried again to lift him. She dared not leave him out here whilst she fetched help, not with the sea so rough and Kurt so defenceless. A particularly rough sea could tip the ship, send his body tumbling into the scuppers, and then the drag of a returning wave could carry him over the side. She gritted her teeth. She must get him back into the interior of the ship.

The sea tilted the deck as she had feared and she clung onto Kurt's shoulders and then, as she saw her mug with the candle inside it tumble across the deck, terror sharpened her brain. She could not lift him, but she could drag him! She seized his booted feet and began to tow his heavily wrapped form across the deck, sliding easily on the ice, until she reached the steel door. She inched it open and backed down the stairs, pulling the doctor behind her. Once she had got him safely inside, lying on the stairs, she closed the door against the cold and the storm. And, of course, the light. Now they were in total darkness again, since her candle and mug were doubtless bobbing about in the sea somewhere, or devoured by fishes. She wondered whether she dare leave him now, for a few moments, whilst she fetched help and a light. Then he slid a few inches further down the stairs and she knew she would have to stay with him. If he fell he could break his neck.

She wanted to make sure that he was still breathing however, despite her somewhat cavalier treatment, so she ran her hands across his chest until she could feel the soft wool of his muffler, and pulled it free of his face. Her fingers sought his lips, his nose. Faintly, his breath warmed her. Sarah uttered a heartfelt sigh. Thank God, he was still alive, the journey across the deck had not harmed him.

Even as she began to relax, though, the ship lurched and the doctor slid down the stairs a little further. Sarah slid her arm, with some difficulty, beneath his broad shoulders, then tried to shift him onto his side so that, if he did begin to slither down the stairs again, she might protect his head, but he was altogether too heavy and broad for the man-oeuvre to be successfully accomplished and what was worse, when she tried to extract her arm, his weight pinned her down as effectively as if he had nailed her to the companionway.

'Doctor! Do wake up!'

He moaned. Sarah had already taken off her muffler so that she could speak clearly; now she pushed back her hood and laid her face against his.

'Kurt? Did you speak? It's me, Sarah.'

A heavy arm came up and wrapped itself round her shoulders. The weight on her heart was lifted, even as she felt herself pulled down on top of her seemingly unconscious patient.

'Doctor? Are you all . . .'

His mouth moved across her face, his lips warm

and very much alive, and found hers. He shifted slightly and her arm came free, but so great was her relief that she made not the slightest attempt to escape. Instead, with a sob of thankfulness, she returned the kiss, then hugged him, gratitude for his obvious recovery swamping every cautious instinct.

The lights, coming on without warning, illumined quite the most passionate kiss ever given by a half-conscious patient to his nurse, Sarah thought. She pulled herself out of his arms and gazed accusingly down at him, but he was clearly far from right. His lids were half-shut and when he raised them to look into her face his eyes had a dreamy, half-focused look.

'What happened? Why were you kissing me, Sarah?'

'Me, kissing you?' Sarah struggled to her knees, her face flaming. 'I did nothing of the sort! You knocked yourself out somehow, on deck, and when the electricity went off I remembered you were up there, and brought you down here. I was trying to bring you round when you suddenly grabbed hold of me and . . . well, you kissed me.'

The doctor blinked and put a hand to his forehead.

'God, my head's splitting. Where is everyone?'

'Probably down in the fishroom, or in the engine room, trying to find out what happened. Look, is it all right to leave you for a minute? I'll get someone to give me a hand to get you along to the sickbay. I can't move you myself, you're too heavy.'

He sat up, his expression still confused, and pushed the hood back off his head. His dark hair stood on end, making him look younger, less sure of himself.

'It's all right, I can manage.' He stood up, wobbled, and clutched at the air. Sarah put out a hand but he waved her back. 'Give me room and I'll make it to my cabin.' He glanced upwards, squinting against the brightness of the newly restored electricity. 'Didn't you say the lights were out?'

'I did. They were.' He reached the end of the companionway and leaned against the bulkhead. His head drooped and she saw that he was swaying on his feet. 'Stay there, Dr Rothwell, and don't dare move!'

Sarah rushed along the corridor and burst into the fishroom. The team members were sitting round a table, sorting through a number of wires and gadgets. Stan looked up as she entered and a guilty expression crossed his face.

'Come to tell me off, Sarah? I'm afraid I had one bright idea too many and overloaded the circuit. We've got the lights working again, but not all the power, I'm afraid.'

Sarah shook her head. 'Never mind about that, Stan, it's the doc. Could you come and give me a hand with him? He fell on the deck and I think he's still concussed, but of course he's sure there's nothing the matter, and . . .'

'I'll come.' Alan Wilde got to his feet. 'You too, Stan, he'll probably listen to you.'

The corridor, when the three of them returned, was empty, but they found Dr Rothwell standing in the middle of the sickbay, looking vaguely round him. Stan took him by the arm.

'Kurt, you've had a fall. Best get to bed.'

The doctor turned to him, his expression puzzled.

'A fall? Me? Nonsense! That's what Sarah said, but I'm perfectly all right and don't have the slightest intention of going to bed.'

'Well, you're going,' Sarah said firmly. 'And what's more, Dr Rothwell, we want to check you over before you sleep. Alan and Stan will get you into your pyjamas, and then we'll check to see you've not fractured anything.' How lovely it would be, she thought, to give orders to Dr Rothwell for a change. 'It won't take long.'

'I don't wear pyjamas,' Dr Rothwell said placidly. 'And I've got work to do. Leave me alone, there's a good girl. I'll just sit down and write up my notes.'

Sarah glanced helplessly at her two companions. She was physically incapable of forcing the doctor to go to bed if he persisted in his refusal, yet she was very sure, by the look in his eyes and the way he moved his head, that he was far from right.

Stan solved the problem, however.

'Sit down, Kurt.' The doctor obeyed, and Stan turned to Sarah. 'Leave us for a few minutes, Nurse.'

Sarah, waiting outside in the corridor, was apprehensive, especially when she heard a roar of rage from the doctor, but presently the door opened and the two men emerged with Dr Rothwell between them. He had been helped out of all his clothing except his trousers.

'Get whatever you need from the sickbay, Sarah,' Stan instructed. 'We'll get Kurt into bed.'

'Very well. Look, can one of you lend him some pyjamas?'

Alan, leading the doctor down the corridor towards his cabin, looked over his shoulder and grinned.

'You don't fancy a naked patient? Okay, we'll do our best.'

And when, presently, Sarah wheeled her trolley into the doctor's cabin, he was lying meekly on the bunk, looking exhausted and drained, and wearing a pair of blue pyjama trousers.

'I found them in his case,' Alan said, when she asked who had lent them. 'I'll give you a hand in looking him over; I've gone through some pretty rigorous first-aid courses, so I've got some idea.'

'Very well, thanks,' Sarah murmured, approaching the bed with considerable caution. 'I'll start with his arms, make sure nothing's broken, though I'm pretty sure his limbs are sound.'

She expected harsh words, if not actual abuse, when she began her examination, but Dr Rothwell behaved completely out of character, doing exactly as she asked with an absent-minded air. As she suspected, there were no broken bones, but he had received a considerable blow on the head.

'There's a three-inch split in his scalp,' she murmured to Alan, as she parted the thick, blood-clotted hair at the back of his head. 'I'll have to clean it out and stitch it. Sutures, I think, it's too big for Steristrip.

Alan looked doubtfully at the ugly gash, then across at Sarah.

'Can you do it, d'you think? It's a pity we don't have ether aboard, that'd keep him quiet.'

Sarah sighed.

'Well, he's very subdued, so perhaps it'll be all right. Can you turn him so that his back is to me, and perhaps he can rest while I shave the hair and clean the wound. Then I'll give him a shot of Lignocaine. Oh, dear!'

She shaved a good patch of scalp around the wound, then picked up the syringe. Her hands were sweating and she leaned over the bed to look down at him. His eyes were closed. Was he asleep or unconscious? Trembling like a leaf, she slid the needle into his scalp, as near to the wound as she dared. He neither moved nor spoke, but as she depressed the plunger he jerked and shouted, frightening Sarah half out of her life, for she thought for one awful moment that he had snapped the needle. But after that one convulsive movement he remained still whilst the rest of the injection was inserted, and Sarah was able to withdraw the needle, secure in the knowledge that she could now put in her sutures without giving her patient pain.

In the end, it proved less fearsome than she had expected. It was a deeper gash than she had at first thought, and also a longer one, but it cleaned up well and it also closed fairly neatly, once she had got over a natural fear that, if she tugged too hard, her patient's ears would end up on top of his head! Once the wound was closed, she turned and grinned at Alan.

'All done. Can you pass me that file? I want to give him an anti-tetanus booster, but I'd best make sure that's the right thing to do. And then I'll put in some Triplopen, I think, just in case there's any risk of infection.'

When she had finished and was putting her trolley straight, she noticed that she was shaking all over. Alan, waiting for the trolley which he intended to push back to the sickbay, noticed too and smiled at her.

'You did marvels, sweetie! Did you notice how speedily poor Stan defected? He can't stand seeing people stitched, apparently.' He took the trolley from her and pushed it out into the corridor. 'I shan't be long. I'll see if I can rustle up a hot cup of tea.'

When the door had closed behind him, Sarah removed her gown and the mask she had worn and turned back to her patient. He was still on his side and seemed to be sleeping soundly. Sarah sighed and ran her fingers through her hair.

'Phew, I wouldn't like to do that every day. He's obviously sound asleep now, but perhaps I ought to give him a shot of something anyway, in case he wakes up in pain.'

'You did very well, Sarah.' Sarah leapt at the sound of that deep, familiar voice. 'I'm proud of you! And I'll sleep like a baby now that it's all over.'

He rolled over on his back, winced a little at the light on his face, then smiled at her.

Sarah felt an absurd desire to burst into tears. He was actually being nice to her, and after she had stitched up his scalp, too!

'I thought you were asleep,' she murmured unsteadily. 'You were very brave considering it was me that was doing it and not a doctor.'

He smiled again, drowsily.

'Grammar, Nurse. It was I! Now go to bed.'

'Not just yet. I'll stay for a little while.' But this time, he really was asleep, she could tell by his heavy breathing and the way his mouth looked. She pulled the covers up over his bare shoulders and chest and fought a stupid desire to bend over and kiss the relaxed mouth. She had never expected to see Kurt Rothwell looking vulnerable, but that was just how he looked now, with the dressing on his head and the bandage none too expertly keeping it in place.

'Is he all right?'

Sarah jumped as Alan spoke. He had re-entered the room noiselessly whilst she was staring down at her patient.

'I think so. I won't leave him, though, because he may feel very rough later, when the Lignocaine wears off. The trouble is, I'm absolutely exhausted after all that tension. I suppose you couldn't bring my bedding in here so that I can sleep on the floor for a couple of hours?'

'No I could not! You go back to your bed and sleep properly for a few hours, and I'll sit in the chair and snooze, and then we'll swop over,' Alan said firmly. 'Lord, do you know it's midnight? Suppose I wake you at four, how would that be?'

'It would be bliss, if you're sure you can stand it,' Sarah admitted. 'And please, Alan, wake me the minute he wakes. Promise?'

Alan patted her cheek.

'I swear it. In fact I'm far too afraid of doing the wrong thing to try anything for myself, so you can go quite happily. Off with you, Sal!'

Sarah took one long, hard look at her patient, then smiled gratefully at Alan.

'You're a brick, Alan, and I'm sorry I ever teased you. Don't forget to wake me at four.'

She made her way to her own cabin and fell into her bunk without bothering to undress. She was asleep as soon as her head touched the pillow.

'Sarah! I'm sorry to wake you, love, but I think I ought.'

Sarah opened leaden lids to find Alan at the door of her cabin. He looked tired and anxious and for a moment she could not imagine why, then it all came flooding back and she shot up in bed, her hands going to her rumpled hair and rumpling it again.

'Glory, is it four o'clock already? I slept like a log. I'll come right away, I'm fully dressed.'

She swung her legs out of the bunk and pushed her feet into her shoes, then stood up.

'Actually, it's seven-thirty,' Alan said apologetically as he led the way to the doctor's cabin. 'I let you sleep on since your patient was asleep too, but he woke about ten minutes ago, in a peevish mood, to put it mildly, and kept trying to get up, so I thought I'd better fetch you.'

Sarah glanced down at herself. Her pale blue jersey was crumped and her navy cords not much better. Her hair was a bird's nest, she had noticed it in her cabin mirror. But she dared not wait to make herself look more presentable, for she had no wish to arrive in the cabin and find that the bird had flown. It might not be beyond her powers to keep Dr Rothwell in bed, but she was very sure that it would be more than she could manage to force him to get back, once he had got himself out.

'You were right, Alan. Are you coming back

with me, or do you want to get some sleep, now? It's well and truly your turn for a rest.'

'If you're sure you can cope, I'll get some sleep. I'm all in.' Alan left her, and Sarah approached Dr Rothwell's cabin cautiously, then straightened her shoulders, knocked perfunctorily on the door panel, and marched into the small room.

'Good morning, Doctor! How do you feel this morning?' She reached for the gown she had worn to stitch the patient's scalp, then let it drop. It was far too crumpled and dirty to add to her consequence.

'A good deal better than you look,' growled the patient ungratefully from his bunk. His eyes were heavy and his face flushed. 'What on earth are you doing in that get-up? You look as if you'd slept in that jumper and those trousers.'

'I did,' Sarah said mildly, reaching for his wrist and then remembering, with annoyance, that she was not wearing uniform and therefore had no fob watch. 'Let me look at your watch, would you?'

'Certainly not!' He was struggling to get out of bed, the flush on his face heightened by temper. 'I'm not ill, girl, I've just had a bang on the head, and you, a trained nurse, dare to come in here looking like . . .'

'All right, I'll fetch Hughie. He'll keep you in bed and talk to you while I make myself respectable.' Sarah, seeing that he was taking no notice of her, put both hands on his shoulders and pushed firmly. He subsided against the pillows, looking astonished. 'See, you're weaker than you thought. Stay there for a moment.'

Hughie was up and beginning to prepare breakfast, but when Sarah explained why she needed him he was anxious to help. He rolled into the small cabin and beamed at the recumbent and glowering Dr Rothwell.

'What's all this then, doc? Our Sarah says . . .'

Sarah did not wait to hear what she was reputed to have said but fled for her cabin. She tore out of her cords and sweater into her uniform, dragged a clean apron out of a drawer and tied it round her, checked that she had her fob watch and her thermometer in its small holder and brushed her hair up into a neat bun. Then she went along to the sickbay and fetched a clean chart and the rest of the paraphernalia needed for doing obs., and hurried back to Dr Rothwell's cabin.

She entered it breathlessly, to find Dr Rothwell leaning back in bed whilst Hughie discoursed about the difficulties of feeding men and cooking for them in seas such as the one which thundered and roared outside at this moment. He also complained that the power supply had not yet been restored to his freezer, so he dared not open it to get anything out for fear that the contents would go bad.

'Absurd it is, doc, when you think how cold it is outside,' he was saying as Sarah crossed the room. 'But food goes off quick, see, in my 'ot kitchen. That Stan!'

Taking advantage of the doctor's apparent calm, Sarah took his wrist and felt for the pulse. She needed no fob watch to tell her that it was a good deal too fast, but she timed it anyway, then took her thermometer out of her top pocket and inserted it in Dr Rothwell's mouth.

Hughie, seeing that she was starting her round,

so to speak, got up and left the room with a cheery wave but the moment he had closed the door behind him, Dr Rothwell's calm deserted him.

'I have *not* got a temperature! I am *not* . . .'

'Be quiet!' She pushed him gently back against the pillows and smiled down into his angry eyes. 'If you've not got a temperature why do you mind me taking it?'

She waited for a nerveracking minute, convinced that he would hurl the thermometer down onto the floor, then took it out. An involuntary squeak escaped her.

'Well? What is it?'

'A hundred and two degrees. I hope that'll convince you that you've simply got to stay in bed.'

'It simply convinces me that you made a hash of whatever you did to me last night,' the doctor said icily. 'My head feels as if it's splitting. I daresay you never thought to sterilise a thing and the wound's probably crawling with streptococci. I feel bloody. I'll have a handful of aspirins and a drink, and then I'm getting out of this bed so that I can see what else you've done.'

Sarah had been standing by the bed looking down at him, her thoughts hideous with the dread that she might have done something to bring this state of affairs about. Now, with his words uttered in such a cold and furious voice, it all proved too much. She turned blindly away from the bunk, tears burning in her eyes. She tried to answer him sensibly, to say that she had taken every precaution before touching the wound, but all that came out was a small, wavery voice saying, with a gulp, 'I'm sorry, I did my best, but . . .'

A pair of very hot arms came round her and a hot face pressed against hers. He had left his bed silently and now he turned her against his naked chest, one hand smoothing her hair, the other holding her close.

'I'm a swine! You poor kid, you did a marvellous job, I'm a bad-tempered . . .'

She pulled away from him, her face wet with tears but her eyes shining.

'Your chest! You were out in that freezing cold with a head injury, and you caught a chest infection! That's why you feel so ill, and why your temperature's up. When you held me then I could hear your chest bubbling away! Get into bed and I'll go through and fetch a course of antibiotics. What would be best for a chest infection, I wonder? Bronchitis, that's what you've got, and Amoxil's good for that.'

He sat down on his bed and swung his legs back in. He was smiling at her.

'Yes, Nurse, I'll do just as you say, Nurse.' She shot across to the door, intent on getting the capsules before he changed his mind and decided that it was her incompetence that had brought on the chest infection. 'Shall I prescribe Amoxil for myself, or do you feel a doctor's unnecessary in the case?'

She stopped, the door open, one hand on the handle.

'You agree, don't you? A course of Amoxil and a good cough mixture—what about Benylin?'

He lay back against the pillows.

'Ideal, Nurse. And a small whisky and lemon, if you please. Patients with bronchitis, may I remind you, are always told to drink a lot. I've got a temperature, too, and we wouldn't want me getting dehydrated.'

'That's true. I'll bring in a jug of coffee.' She smiled demurely at his groan. 'I can tell you're going to prove an ideal patient, Dr Rothwell!'

CHAPTER EIGHT

DR ROTHWELL was not a good patient, but after that first, traumatic morning, Sarah managed to keep him in bed and, if not contented, at least not so furious that he ignored her treatment.

On the third day of his illness she went into the cabin at eight o'clock, with his breakfast tray balanced on one arm, wearing her freshly laundered uniform. She clicked the light on and turned towards his bunk. He had been woken earlier, when Stan took him a cup of tea, but had obviously dropped back to sleep again. Now, he stretched, winced as his head-wound touched the top of the bunk, and turned to eye her appraisingly.

'Good morning, Nurse. Is there a real breakfast on that tray or are you going to try to get me to eat more slops?'

'It's a fairly real breakfast,' Sarah said cautiously, putting her tray down on the small table beside the bunk. 'I haven't taken your temperature yet, so it isn't bacon and egg, or sausage and tomatoes, but . . .'

He sat up, then stretched again. Despite her suggestions that he might like to wear both halves of his pyjamas, he was naked from the waist up and would, Sarah suspected, have been naked from the waist down as well, left to his own devices.

'Then why not take my temperature this minute, because I'm starving.' He turned a pathetic eye on

her. 'Are you trying to starve me into good behaviour, Sarah?'

'Of course not. Eat up your nice porridge and
you'll feel much better.' Sarah pulled the table
across the bunk, for it was on a swivel, and straightened the tray. 'There you are!'

'Look, woman . . .' his tone usually became less
pathetic, she told herself, when he realised that he
was not about to get his own way. 'I'm not eating
this pap unless you'll swear it can be followed by a
decent meal. My belly's flapping against my back-
bone after days of your invalid cookery.'

'What a horrible expression, Doctor!' Sarah
sighed and took out her thermometer. 'Well, you
do look a lot better. Did you take your capsule with
your early morning tea? Amoxil is best . . .'

'. . . taken on an empty stomach,' he finished, his
voice sarcastic. 'Don't ask patients questions when
you've just filled their mouths with loathsome ther-
mometers, woman!'

'Right.' Sarah stood silently watching her fob
watch for longer than strictly necessary, knowing
that the delay would annoy her victim, then took it
out and gazed at it, lips pursed.

'Well? Damn it, Sarah, I *know* I've not got a
fever! If you don't fetch me something substantial
to eat I'm getting out of this bed and going to the
galley myself.'

'Oh, very well, since your temperature is normal.' Sarah picked up the porridge. 'What's it to
be?'

Dr Rothwell took the porridge from her.

'This first, then bacon, egg, sausage, a round of
fried bread, a few fried potatoes if Hughie's got any

cold ones left over from dinner, some baked beans, and plenty of toast and marmalade.' Dr Rothwell began to demolish the porridge with zest. 'That'll do me, I think.'

'It would do *for* you, if I were foolish enough to let you eat that lot,' Sarah said austerely. 'I daresay bacon and egg wouldn't hurt you, though.' She left the cabin and presently returned, with a plate on which two rashers of bacon flanked a golden-centred fried egg. 'Will this do?'

'Yes, to be going on with.' He took the plate from her, then gave her a quick, glinting grin. 'Sorry, but I've got a big frame to support and hunger makes me tend to bite the hand that doesn't feed me!'

'It's all right.' She got out her pen and took the chart from the end of the bed, filling in the temperature reading. 'I do like a nice, tidy ward! I'm not going to bother with your b.p. today, but I suppose I ought to ask . . . Well, I can't help noticing . . .'

'What's the matter, Nurse?' Dr Rothwell, eyeing her hot face, gave a malicious grin. 'Surely there's nothing a professional like you minds mentioning? I *am* a doctor, after all!'

'Oh, I know, it's just . . . Here, fill it in yourself!' Sarah handed him the chart. 'Especially that column.' She indicated it with the tip of her biro.

'Oh, you're interested in the good old bowel movements, are you, Nurse?' His voice was smooth but she could hear the unholy amusement at the back of it. 'Now let me see, when did I last ask for a bedpan?'

'You haven't, and well you know it,' Sarah snapped. 'I could give you an enema, I suppose, but there's always castor oil. Or suppositories.'

'Pax, you hit below the belt,' Dr Rothwell said hastily, and grinned at her giggle. 'Ill though I am, I do still wield a certain amount of power aboard this ship! The men take turns to come along during the watches when you aren't around, and they've been helping me along the corridor. Though the way I feel now, it won't be necessary after today. Because I'll humour you so far, Sarah, and no further.'

Sarah sat down on his bed.

'What do you mean by that?'

'My temperature's down, and I'm getting up!'

'Yes, of course you are. But not today. Not quite yet.'

His fork, halfway to his mouth, froze, whilst a scowl descended.

'Yes, Nurse. Yes today, yes quite today.'

Sarah watched as he began to eat again. She knew that he was not yet fit enough to leave his bed, let alone to start the gruelling round of work which he would immediately undertake. But how to stop him?

'Doctor, I really don't think you should get up for another forty-eight hours. Just give the capsules a chance. How would it be if I . . . what's the matter with the bacon?'

'Nothing.' He lay knife and fork down on the plate and leaned back. 'I'm a little weary, that's all. Not used to such a big meal. Don't bother with the toast and marmalade.

A weight was lifted from Sarah's shoulders. He knew he was weak still, but his masculine superiority would not allow him to admit it! She took the plate, still half full, away and put it on the floor by the bunk.

'Drink your coffee before it gets cold, Doctor.'

He opened his eyes, sighed, and reached for his cup.

'What a bully you are, Nurse Barford! Just wait until I'm on my feet again!'

'Where are you off to now, Sarah? You're always in a rush. My head aches—why can't you come and talk to me for a bit?'

It was late evening on the fifth day of the doctor's enforced rest, and he was fretful, hot, complaining of aches and pains, saying that his evening meal had been too heavy, that his capsules gave him indigestion, that his work was being neglected.

'I don't mind talking. But earlier, you said I nagged you, and before that, that I must be neglecting my typing. So I thought if I wasn't here I couldn't be nagging you, but I could be doing my typing. See?' Nevertheless, Sarah walked over and sat on his bed. 'The trouble with you, Dr Rothwell, is that you don't know what you *do* want!'

He took her hand and stroked between the fingers, looking up into her face, his expression remorseful. Sarah's heart turned over. She found his sweetness even more difficult to handle than his bad temper.

'I know what I want, all right, but it wouldn't be good for me to have it! Oh, don't blush, my lovely, or I'll get right out of this bed and give you a reason for blushing.' He released her fingers and sighed. 'I want to get on with my work, and write up my notes, and yet I've got sufficient sense to know that if I try to run before I can walk it'll make things difficult for everyone. So I get edgy, and bored, and then I take it out on you. Forgive me, Nurse?'

'Of course,' she smiled at him. 'If there's one thing nurses do understand, it's the impatience of patients!'

He leaned back against his pillows.

'Good. Tell me about yourself, Sarah. I know nothing about you, you know. Why aren't you married, with babies round you?'

Sarah shrugged.

'Too busy learning my profession, perhaps. I'm one of a big family, you know.'

He raised his brows. The languid look lifted for a moment.

'I don't know. Tell me!'

Sarah told him. About her father, a farmer, and her mother, a placid housewife. About her three sisters, Penny, Susan and Philippa, all married to farmers, all older than she, all with small children. About the hardships of living with parents who, loving though they were, did not think that daughters needed to leave home or have careers.

'The others never wanted to go, you see,' Sarah admitted ruefully. 'And there was I, the baby, determined to leave home, become a nurse, and see the world. I think my sisters thought I was a changeling, and my poor mother, who's so placid herself, could only wonder where she'd gone wrong. Especially after I told Jack Winters that I wouldn't marry him if he was the last man on earth!'

'Who's Jack Winters? No, don't tell me, he's a farmer.'

Sarah laughed and nodded.

'Very true. And what's worse, his farm is next to ours, and he actually owns it, he's not a tenant or anything, and he seemed so ideal to Mother and Father. But I couldn't do it, you know, not even for my family, so I upped and offed, and Jack married a townie who thinks getting up at five to milk the cows is glamorous, and that mud's good for the complexion.'

'Well, well, well! Who'd have thought our little Sarah was a career girl.' His glance was speculative, bringing warmth to Sarah's cheeks. 'I suppose you're set on ruling some hospital eventually, and scaring all the doctors into instant obedience?'

'Not at all. I want to nurse aboard a cruise ship, or go to the Caribbean with a rich patient, or . . . well, I want to see the world. I don't want to crumble away.'

He gave her a sardonic glance.

'I see. And marriage is the equivalent of crumbling away? Is that what you mean?'

'Of course not, marriage isn't in question as such, I was talking about marrying Jack and settling down in a sea of mud, in the spot where I'd spent my entire life up to then.'

'Then you don't object to marriage, if you find the right man?'

Where was all this leading? Sarah stared down at her fingers and tried to think of the right answer. She didn't want him to run away with the impression that all her nursing career and her intention of seeing the world boiled down to a search for the right man.

'I want to marry one day. But not until I've had some fun.' She raised her eyes to his face. 'What about you, Dr Rothwell? What's your ambition? Anyway, now I come to think of it, *you* aren't married, and you're *much* older than me!'

'If you think I'm going to lie here and let you into the secrets of my past, you're mistaken.' He took her hand and turned it over, palm uppermost. 'What nice hands you've got, not all practical and square-tipped, like some nurses!'

She jerked her hand out of his grasp.

'Don't prevaricate. Why haven't you married?'

He shrugged.

'I nearly have, twice. I'm thirty-three now though, so I don't think I'll keep my freedom for very much longer, somehow.'

A tiny chill crept across Sarah's skin, goose-fleshing it.

'Why not? Have you someone in mind?'

'Yes.'

The coldness crept further. There was something so final in the brusque monosyllable. The question and answer game had lost its savour, she had no urge to ask about the woman in his life, all she wanted was to get away from him, and give herself time to think how fortunate it was that she had not fallen irrevocably in love with him, how happy she was that his occasional attacks of good temper and charm had been of short duration!

'Well, I'm sure I hope you'll be very happy.' She got to her feet. 'I've got to go and do some work, now. I'll come and settle you down in about an hour.'

She left the room briskly and went along to the sickbay, but for all her good intentions there was very little work to do, until he was able to write up

more of his notes. She sat down at her desk and
checked through her own notes, then decided to
write a nice, long letter to her parents. She would
post it just as soon as they reached their home port
once more.

'I think you might get up tomorrow, Dr Rothwell.
That is, if you promise not to do anything foolish,
like going up on deck.'

Sarah stood by his bed, looking down at him. It
had been a full week, but there was no doubt that
he was very much better. He was eating normally,
sleeping soundly, working on his notes, and the
head wound was healing beautifully.

'Good girl, my own diagnosis exactly.' He had
been reading, but he laid the book down on the
bedside table. 'I'll get up for breakfast on the mess
deck, I think, and you can report to me in the
sickbay at nine o'clock precisely.'

Sarah smiled but shook a reproving finger at him.

'You'll never frighten me quite the same again,
sir, not now I've nursed you! And I'd just like to say
that I've never had a worse patient, or one who was
more difficult to please.'

He grinned at her, patently unrepentant.

'Nonsense, you found me a charming patient,
you just don't like to admit it. And as for never
being afraid of me again—want to bet?'

'That freezer's never been right, not since Stan
mucked about with the electricity supply,' Hughie
muttered, anxiously inspecting the contents of his
freezer. 'I open it once a day, so's the cold is

contained, and if I forget to fetch something out, that's too bad.'

It was Sarah's afternoon off and she was in the kitchen, making a birthday cake for Stan, who would be thirty-three the next day. It was a special cake, her own recipe, and it needed a good deal of chocolate, several grated oranges, and a fluffy, coffee-flavoured filling. Glancing round the galley, in fact, it would not have been difficult to guess that a birthday was in prospect, for Alan had been making crackers from red crepe paper in one corner and, in addition to Sarah's cake, they had made several large trays of fancy cakes, which would be iced next day.

'Well, don't miss anything for the birthday tea,' Sarah urged, as Hughie backed out of the freezer. 'I take it you're defrosting the raspberries and cream now?'

'Aye, that's right.' Hughie tipped a number of packets into a big yellow bowl on the table. 'Any road, there's a second chance tomorrow. Not that we ought to pamper that Stan—whose fault is it that my freezer ain't in good nick, eh?'

'Poor Stan,' Sarah began to pour the mixture into an immense cake tin. 'What are you serving for dinner, when the birthday tea's over?'

Hughie frowned.

'This is a trawler, gal, not the *Queen Mary*! We'll eat the cake and the fancies instead of a pudding, after dinner. You can't go serving seamen with afternoon tea.' He snorted. 'You'll be expecting me to make cucumber and salmon sandwiches next!'

'I see. Then why the raspberries and cream?'

'Stan's favourite grub, seemingly. We'll have 'em before that fancy cake of yours. I'll do some short-bread, too, so's the crew can soak the biscuits in the raspberry juice, otherwise they won't feel well-filled.'

'My God, Hughie, those men are fed like Stras-bourg geese,' Sarah protested, staggering oven-wards with her heavy tin. 'I'm jolly glad you never got a job as cook at the General, or all the nurses would be rolling around weighing about twenty stone!' She turned from the oven, wiping her hot face. 'Gracious, I could do with a nice, long show-er! But instead of that, I'm going down to the sickbay to type up all the work Dr Rothwell left me.'

'I thought it was your afternoon off,' Hughie said, putting the mixing bowl into the sink. 'You don't want to work on your afternoon off.'

'I know, and don't breathe a word to Dr Roth-well, but since tomorrow is a special sort of dinner, I'm going to stop work early and give myself a good pampering, have a shower, do my hair, that sort of thing. And then I'll be looking my best for the dinner. But of course I couldn't do that unless I did the extra work this afternoon. See?' She moved towards the door. 'I'll come back in two hours to check on my cake, but could you be a dear and take a look about thirty minutes before it's due to come out? I've never cooked such a big one before.'

'I thought you and the doc were getting on like a house on fire ever since his bump on the head,' Hughie protested. 'So why not just tell him you want to stop early?'

'Because, dear Hughie, we only get on like

houses on fire when I do exactly—but *exactly*—
what I'm told. If I asked for time off, he'd mutter
about special privileges, or accuse me of wanting to
look pretty for . . . for one of the men. Or he might,
so I'm not taking any more chances.'

'Point taken. You'll pop in tomorrow after
lunch, then, to ice the fancies? One thing I'll grant
you, you're a dab hand with an icing gun.'

'Okay. As for being good with the gun, that's all
my practise with a syringe, I expect. See you,
Hughie!'

She left him washing up.

Promptly at two o'clock on Stan's birthday afternoon, Sarah headed for the showers. The cake was
iced and ready, the raspberries unfrozen, and the
cream whipped to perfection. All that remained,
she told herself, was for her to spend an enjoyable
couple of hours getting herself ready for the dinner.

She slipped into the shower room, hung her silk
dressing gown behind the door of her favourite
shower, and glanced carefully at the other cubicles.
They were empty. On one occasion, when she first
came aboard, she had been in the embarrassing
position of finding herself the only female in the
showers whilst, around her, a very frank conversation about women ashore went on between three
crew members. Since that never-to-be-forgotten
occasion, she had been careful to choose the right
time for her ablutions, speedily learning that direct-
ly before and after a watch came off was bad, as was
the early evening before dinner, when the team
usually descended on the showers.

However, she had chosen right this time, it

seemed, and was to be a solitary showerer once again. She locked her little door, then ran the water and undressed, throwing her dirty clothing beneath the spray as she wriggled out of each garment. It was her practice to wash her clothes in the shower and then to take them back and dry her undies in her own cabin and her heavier clothing in the galley, as the men did.

Presently, when she was naked, she knelt down and washed her clothes with soap powder, then rinsed and wrung them, and finally put them into the plastic carrier bag she had brought for the purpose and stepped into the shower herself.

It was glorious to feel the hot water sluicing down on her cleaning off the stickiness caused by icing the cakes, and the effect of being bundled up in heavy clothing for sixteen hours a day. She would give herself the full treatment this afternoon—and not before time, when she remembered the rapid showers and scanty make up which had sufficed lately. In honour of Stan's birthday, she intended to look her best. With this object, she lathered herself from the tip of her head to her toes and then stood, face upturned, and rinsed herself thoroughly beneath the stream of water. When she was glowing, she resolutely turned the shower to cool and then to cold, leaping out with a muffled shriek when she felt she could stand no more. Then she turned the water off and towelled herself briskly, until she was glowing again, and full of well-being.

Talcum powder was applied generously, whilst she hummed a tune to herself, then she aimed a perfume spray at her pulse points and brushed out her hair. Finally, she cleaned the little room thoroughly and put on her silk dressing gown, tying it firmly round her small waist.

There was a mirror in the shower, and she coaxed her hair into the deep, natural waves and curls into which it fell when unrestricted, and then glanced approvingly at her reflection. To be sure, the silk gown clung in an exceedingly provocative fashion to breasts and hips, but then no one was going to see her in the short sprint along the corridor, and her skin was glowing with health, her hair shining with its recent wash. She was about to step into the corridor, in fact, when she heard the slam of the steel door which led onto the deck.

Sarah hesitated. She had taken so long over her shower that the team were coming down to the fishroom, or possibly even heading for the mess deck, because Hughie always served tea and biscuits to anyone off watch there around this time. She glanced down at herself again. Silk is silk, she told herself ruefully, and it might be better not to meet Dr Rothwell face to face in the corridor in such a clinging garment. He would undoubtedly think that she was hoping to meet one of the men, or even if he did not actually go that far, he would accuse her of carelessness in not making sure she was alone before walking the corridor clad in such a revealing garment.

The sounds outside were fading into silence. She waited until she could hear no sound at all, then slipped out of the door and set off up the corridor, towards the haven of her own cabin.

She was barely two steps on her way, however, when Alan appeared, coming from the direction of his own cabin. He had a towel in one hand and was plainly making for the showers. He saw her and whistled appreciatively.

'Hey-ey-ey! That's a very sexy garment!'

Horribly embarrassed, Sarah followed his glance and saw once again how the silk moulded the outline of her breasts and nipples, looking almost as revealing as complete nakedness.

'I'm getting ready for dinner,' she said defensively. 'If you want a shower, the place is empty.'

Alan moved closer. She could not reach her cabin without passing him, and he was standing in the very middle of the corridor, effectively blocking it, with a hand on either bulkhead. He was looking at her in a way she found almost frightening, it was such a hot and hungry look.

'Do move, Alan!' Her voice came out a little higher than usual. 'I can't get to my cabin with you there.'

'Why not try? I'll probably let you through.'

His eyes roamed across her with such sensuous interest that it was like being touched. Sarah felt the colour flood her face and held her ground. She must be brisk!

'Don't be silly, Alan. Do move!'

He dropped one arm and stood to one side, leaving a small gap through which she could squeeze. She made a dart for it and found herself trapped, with Alan's chest against her silk-clad breasts, his hands framing her face.

'If you want to pass, a kiss is the price!'

It was no joke, he meant it. His mouth was moving and his eyes burned down at her. His hands slid down the sides of her neck, one going to her nape to control her, the other sliding down inside her silk dressing gown, the fingers hot on her talcum-smooth flesh, scented and still warm from the shower.

'Alan, stop it, I don't . . .'

He lunged forward and his mouth fastened on hers. She tried to jerk away and the hand on the nape of her neck pressed, forbidding escape. She tried to kick but he was too close, and when she struggled the hand inside her dressing gown moved, so that she remembered the gown was merely wrapped over, and that if it was roughly handled it would just undo and fall open. She froze. But even as Alan's mouth began to work on hers, they were interrupted by a voice saying crisply: 'May I pass?'

Alan let her go as if she had been red-hot and stepped back so that she was no longer crushed between him and the bulkhead, waving Dr Rothwell through, but the doctor made no attempt to pass them. Instead he gave them a long, icy look.

'This, Wilde, is neither the time nor the place for a seduction scene. As for you, Nurse . . .'

Alan grinned uneasily. His face was patched with red and there was sweat on his cheekbones. Sarah saw that his good looks and poise had both deserted him.

'Seduction, Kurt? Damn it, it was only a kiss! What's a kiss?'

'In that case, why don't you kiss Dr Rothwell?' Sarah said sarcastically. 'After all, Alan, you said the price of being allowed to walk along the corridor was a kiss, but you've not tried to extract one from him!'

'Oh, I see, Alan was just teaching you an old

shipboard custom, was he?' Dr Rothwell's tone was frankly sceptical. 'Are you trying to tell me, Sarah, that it's a case of kissing when you pass in the corridor? In that case . . .' He grabbed Sarah and for the second time in five minutes she found herself helpless in a man's arms. 'Let's hope the rest of the team don't reappear and want to come past, or you aren't ever going to get dressed!'

'Let me go!' Sarah felt she had suffered enough for her stupidity in wearing nothing but the silk gown. 'Please, Doctor, this is past a joke!'

'You're quite right. Off with you!' He turned her towards her cabin, giving her silk-clad bottom an unnecessarily hearty slap. 'I'll see you presently, Sarah. And now, Wilde, you and I are going to have a few words!'

Sarah thought that she had never got dressed more quickly, with her attention focused on the door of her cabin, certain that at any moment Dr Rothwell would knock and come in, to give her a piece of his mind. But, in fact, she was fully dressed and had done her hair before the expected knock came.

'Sarah? Come along to the sickbay as soon as you're ready, would you?'

'I'll be there, sir.'

Sarah eyed herself critically in the mirror. She was wearing the low-cut, blue Indian muslin dress, and she knew very well how it suited her though she had not worn it since her first night aboard. It emphasised the whiteness of her skin, and the dark fire of her hair. She put up her chin. Object if you must, Kurt Rothwell, but I'm not on duty now, and it is a party, she thought defiantly, heading for the sickbay.

She entered the room, to find the doctor sitting behind the desk and eyeing her with a mixture of amusement and exasperation. She hoped, devotedly, that the amusement would remain uppermost during the interview which was to follow.

'Sit down, Sarah.' He waited until she was seated, and then continued: 'You'll notice that I'm not calling you by your title, but that doesn't mean I'm not annoyed with you, it merely means that I'm not annoyed with you in any professional sense.'

'What a relief,' Sarah said crossly. 'Does that mean my stupidity in getting trapped and kissed by Alan won't go down in the book you're keeping against me?'

He frowned. 'Don't be silly. What I wanted to say to you was that you're not taking Wilde seriously, and you should. He's extremely susceptible, you know, and not used to being found as resistible as you say you find him. That gown, my dear child, was fatal! It didn't need much imagination to see that you'd not got a stitch underneath it, and there really is no need to wander round the ship dressed—or undressed—like that. Hell, Sarah, see it from my point of view. I'll have trouble on my hands if you get him so worked up that he bursts into your cabin and tries to . . .'

'It was a mistake,' Sarah said quickly. 'Honestly, sir, a mistake! I had my shower, and I'd washed my jeans and sweater because I knew I was putting on nice clean stuff. So then all I had was my dressing gown, and I put that on and planned to come out when the team had gone to their rooms. I waited until it was quiet and sneaked out, only Alan was heading for the showers. The rest you know. And I really don't see why I should dress like a nun just because Alan thinks he's irresistible!'

'Very well, point taken. But the question is, Sarah, how do you really feel about Alan? I spoke to him pretty roughly, I don't mind telling you, and he was indignant, said he was sure you liked him. He more or less accused me of being jealous, trying to keep you two apart. If this is even remotely true, for God's sake tell me, and you can carry on as much as you like, only kindly do so in private.'

Sarah sighed and rolled her eyes ceilingwards.

'I swear by Almighty God that I will speak the truth, the whole truth . . . Dr Rothwell, I'm not in the slightest bit interested in Alan. Please be convinced, because it happens to be true. All I want, at the moment, is the chance to get on with the job I'm doing. And I want to keep the friendships I've already made intact. Is that crystal clear?'

He was smiling, actually looking approvingly at her.

'I'm glad to hear it. Then do your best to keep a good distance between yourself and Wilde and we'll brush through the whole business without too many egos being smashed. We're steaming for home now, you know that, don't you?'

Sarah laughed and got to her feet.

'Do I know it? The grins on the faces of the crew would have told me, even if nothing else had! Can I go now, Doctor, and put the finishing touches to my appearance so that I dazzle Stan at his birthday dinner?'

He stood up too, and came round the desk towards her.

'Right.' He put a hand on her shoulder, then moved it up, to gently caress her cheek. 'You're a good girl, Sarah. I'm sorry if my attitude has seemed harsh, but it's been for everyone's good.'

'I'll try to bear it in mind, sir.' She could feel her heartbeat speeding up under the touch of his fingers, knew her cheek was warming into rose. She subdued a very improper desire to rest against his broad chest and to tell him that though Alan did not interest her in the slightest . . .

'Off with you, then! I'll see you at dinner.'

He turned towards the desk and she left the room, reminding herself that he had told her he had someone in mind when it came to marrying. She wondered if he loved the woman, or if she was just 'suitable'. But it was no concern of hers. She turned into her cabin, then turned straight round and went out again. She would see whether Stan needed any help to get into the suit he kept boasting he had brought aboard, or if Hughie had everything ready. And whilst she did so, she would let drop a hint or two about Dr Rothwell's woman. Not that she cared, of course, but it would be interesting to find out what sort of woman *did* manage to please him!

CHAPTER NINE

THE birthday party had been a great success. The food was good, everyone was in an excellent humour, and Dr Rothwell produced a crate of champagne from the bowels of the ship and they all drank to Stan and to the success of the voyage, though this seemed assured, for the information which they had acquired pleased everyone and the Skipper could not praise highly enough the new ice-fighting techniques which the team had developed.

Sarah's cake, too, had been pronounced delicious, and she had been kissed soundly by Stan, who held her in his one good arm and, after three glasses of champagne, talked about his wife and children in a wistful manner which made Sarah feel quite homesick for her own family.

The following day, however, all was not so well. Sarah went to the galley at lunchtime to find Hughie banging around, in a rousing temper.

'Hello, Hughie? What's the matter?'

Hughie turned from the sink and sent a plate skidding viciously across the draining board.

'It's the bloody freezer, that's what's wrong. Never been right since Stan's mucking about with the electric, I said so, didn't I? I went and got the food out for tonight, same as always, I was defrosting a big joint of pork, as nice a joint as you could wish for. Only . . . Well, see for yourself.'

He gestured to the top of the fridge. There, on a plate, appearing to eye her balefully, was a pig's head.

Sarah laughed.

'Oh, Hughie, what an awful thing to happen! But why can't you open the freezer again and get out something different? I know you think you shouldn't, but we haven't got all that long aboard now, surely? I mean, if one little piece of meat went bad as a result, then we wouldn't starve, with only another ten days or so at sea.'

Hughie, normally so even-tempered, scowled at her.

'Use your sense girl, isn't it! No time there is left now to defrost a joint. Something else we shall have to eat, but the dear knows what!'

Sarah noticed how Welsh his accent had suddenly become, and knew that he was truly distressed. He was proud of his reputation as the best cook in the fleet, and reluctant to be a laughing stock.

'Well, all right then, something else. What do you have? Surely there must be some suitable tinned meat?'

Hughie shook his head. 'None that I can spare, love. The fact is, I always get in sufficient meat— corned beef, ham and the like—to feed the men on the last day at sea, when the galley fire's been put out and the ship is being fettled up.' He shook his fist at the pig's head. 'That damned thing! Well wrapped it was, just like a decent joint, and of course I got it out and what with Stan's party and all, never so much as a glance did I give it. And now, when it's too late, it sits there grinning at me!'

'That is unfortunate, but surely there must be . . . Oh! Hughie, I've got it!'

'What? Tell me, so's we can start.'

But Sarah, smiling mischievously, shook her head.

'I can't tell you, not for a moment. I'll just nip out though, and then I'll come back and we'll work on it.'

She left the galley and went straight along to the fish room, where she knew some of the men were working. Her luck was in. Alan and Albert, the marine biologists, were there, one writing notes, the other drawing pictures of what appeared to be a mass of squiggling worms. Sarah interrupted them without compunction.

'I say, how's the krill situation?'

'Good as ever.' Alan smiled. He had taken his dismissal very lightly, she considered, and behaved with courtesy and friendliness towards her. 'Why? Want to try some?'

Sarah pulled a face.

'Personally, no, but needs must! It's true that you two consider it absolutely safe and a marvellous source of protein, isn't it?'

Two heads nodded.

'And that everyone on board, just about, has said they *will* try it, one day. Only that day never seems to come?'

Once again, the biologists nodded simultaneously.

'Great! Tonight's the night, chaps! How much can you let us have?'

Alan and Albert exchanged a bemused glance. Alan spoke first.

'About a ton, if you like, but . . .'

'Don't say Kurt's seen our point of view at last. By all that's wonderful . . .'

'Well, no, the day of miracles isn't that far advanced,' Sarah admitted. 'I'm afraid krill is instead of roast pork, due to a slight blunder.' She outlined the sad story of Hughie and the pig's head. 'So you see,' she finished. 'Now's the chance for us to try the krill, and no one any the wiser until it's eaten. It couldn't have a better try-out now, could it?'

'I'll grant you that,' Albert said dubiously. 'But suppose they guess? Or hate it?'

'Oh, we'll cross that bridge when we come to it. Hughie and I are such wonderful cooks that they probably won't know it isn't pâté de fois gras, or river salmon. Come on, hand some over.'

There was an immense refrigerator against one wall. Alan walked over to it and pulled out a sack. He handed it to Sarah.

'There you are, all clean and sorted. Take it away and do your worst.' He turned to Albert. 'I feel an acute attack of vegetarianism coming on.'

'No you don't!' Sarah protested, taking the bag with some caution. 'No shirking! We're *all* going to try the krill. And don't breathe a word to a soul, or we'll have half of the cowards pretending they're not hungry.'

She left the room and hurried back to the galley, dumping the bag down in the middle of the scrubbed kitchen table.

'There! Take a look.'

'That's krill, isn't it?' Hughie said, opening the neck of the bag and peering inside. 'Phew, what a niff!'

'Nonsense, it'll be delicious!' Sarah peered over his shoulder. 'They are dead, aren't they? Those little shrimpy things, I mean?'

''Course they are. Smell as if they've been dead a week,' Hughie said succinctly. 'Oh well, I daresay we can make something of it. We could do a chowder, and then dried egg omelettes.'

'No, that's too easy,' Sarah protested. 'I vote for salmon cutlets. We can use . . .'

The conversation became culinary and presently the two of them began to work.

Within minutes of assembling for dinner, Sarah could tell that Dr Rothwell was in a temper. He talked readily enough to other members of the team, laughed, had a couple of drinks, but whenever she glanced towards him his eyes seemed to be upon her with an expression of brooding fury in their depths. She wondered whether he had heard a rumour of the forthcoming krill, or whether he had found a mistake in her books; something was obviously very wrong.

She voiced her thoughts aloud to Hughie as she went through into the galley to help him serve the tomato soup.

'Could the doc have discovered about the krill, Hughie? He keeps giving me nasty looks.'

'Oh, you and your imagination! Why on earth . . .' Hughie broke off. 'You shouldn't have kept it from the doc though, gal, seeing as he's in charge. Was that why you dodged behind my fridge and hid yourself away when he come in during the afternoon, looking for you?'

'Of course. Why else? That man's only got to

look at me to know the secrets of my soul, and I want him to taste the krill with an unprejudiced palate,' Sarah said. 'Anyway, it won't hurt anyone and the die's cast. I'll tell the chaps to line up for their soup.'

She ate her soup as quickly as she could, and watched Alan and Albert make a meal of theirs, with several bread rolls to fill them up. She caught Alan's eye and mouthed 'you dare!' at him, and giggled at his expression. Dr Rothwell's icy glance swept over them and she subsided in her seat. Curse the man, could she not even smile without incurring his displeasure?

'Everyone finished? There's curry to follow, with rice and chutney. And cod cutlets in shrimp sauce for anyone who doesn't like curry.' Sarah smiled sweetly round the table. 'Who's for curry?'

As she had guessed, everyone was. Even Albert and Alan, with relieved smirks, opted for it. They thought, of course, that the cod cutlets with shrimp sauce would be the krill. And they were right, only the curry was krill too. After a good hour of experimentation, Hughie had declared that the only thing which would even partially mask the strong, oily flavour of the tiny shrimps was 'a good, 'ot curry', so they had concocted just that.

Sarah watched as the men lifted their forks and began to eat the food. At first, no one noticed anything. Then conversation began to falter. Stan, who had been shovelling curry in at great speed, delighted to have a meal he could eat with one hand, began to prod curiously at the curry.

'Odd, I adore curry, but this has got a funny taste.' He turned to Sarah. 'Been helping Hughie, lass? What meat did he use? Not whale, I suppose?'

One by one, the men stopped chewing and regarded their plates with a sort of horrified fascination. Dr Rothwell put his knife and fork down with a clatter.

'Krill!' He pushed his plate away. 'Whose idea was this? Come clean, Sarah. I saw you smirking just now—I suppose this is your idea of a joke? Or should I say yours and Alan's? If so, I don't think much of your sense of humour and less of your abilities as a cook. It's poisonous!'

'It isn't, it's perfectly edible,' Sarah protested weakly, pushing her own plate thankfully away. 'The Japanese love it, you know they do.'

The doctor's brows rose. 'Indeed? Then why is it that the Japanese are using krill only for farm feeding stuffs and for manuring the land?'

'But you said they ate it! You said they fished vast quantities out of the sea and used it.'

'That was all past tense, my dear child. The Japanese housewives tried the stuff but they didn't care for it at all, and not the most seductive advertising could take away their dislike of the actual taste. So now the stuff's not used for food production at all, or not for human beings, at any rate.'

'She's been feeding us manure,' Stan said disgustedly. 'Well, I call that a bit thick! You want a good spanking, Sarah.'

'You all kept saying you'd try krill some time, and now you have,' Sarah said crossly. 'And don't exaggerate, Stan, it's only animal feeding stuff.' Unable to resist the temptation, she added righteously. 'The manure's coming on next!'

Someone cuffed her teasingly, and there were

cries of 'Make her eat her curry!' and 'feed her to the fishes, fellows!' but they were all in good part. Only Dr Rothwell continued to look outraged and furious as Hughie brought in a huge jam pudding. As soon as the pudding had been served, he leaned across the table and spoke to Sarah.

'In future, Nurse Barford, will you kindly inform me before you try experiments of any kind on my team? I refuse to risk the men's lives twice over—it's enough to have to face Arctic conditions without facing your cookery too.'

The men thought it was all part of the joke but Sarah favoured the doctor with her iciest look, then got to her feet.

'Extra jam, anyone?'

The disastrous meal was over and most of the team were thinking about their beds when Sarah went into the galley to make herself a hot drink before seeking her own couch. Hughie, watching her in the firelight, smiled sympathetically as she raided the biscuit tin.

'Bit peckish, are you? Was it you cast up accounts after the krill, then?'

'Ask me no questions and I'll tell you no lies,' Sarah said, munching a biscuit. 'If I was sick, it was from tension and not from krill. You should have been on the mess deck after dinner! I tell you, I don't know whether it was just the krill or whether there was something else, but wrathful Rothwell gave me no peace! He sniped and snarled and made bad jokes at my expense and every time I looked up his cold and steely eye was upon me. I became convinced that he knew some awful secret about me that no one else knew, and was about to blow the gaffe. It made me so nervous I was sick.'

'Go on,' Hughie said comfortably. 'What could he know about you? An open book you are, gal!'

'Yes, I am. He couldn't know anything, really. It was just the way he kept glaring at me. He can be downright sinister at times.'

'Well, it'll all be forgot by the morning,' Hughie said. 'Go you off to bed now, gal, and forget the krill. Take your cup of cocoa and some of them biscuits and a good book, and it'll be tomorrow before you know it. And if you treat me right, I'll let you make a treacle pud tomorrow. That'll make 'em forgive you for the krill.' He smiled fatly at her. 'I've defroze a leg of lamb, too. They all like lamb.'

'Saved by a treacle pud! Thanks, Hughie.' Sarah blew him a kiss and opened the galley door, with her mug of cocoa in one hand. 'Sweet dreams!'

She glanced up and down the corridor, but there was no one in sight. It was not terribly late, but she felt she needed a good night's rest. It would be a relief, she knew, simply to get away from Dr Rothwell's basilisk stare.

She entered her cabin, clicked the light on, and put her cocoa and the biscuits down on the table by the bunk. Then she undressed, washed at the handbasin, and slipped into a flimsy blue nightie. She was sitting before the mirror, vigorously brushing out her hair, when she heard the knock at the door.

'Wait a moment!' She jumped to her feet and was slipping into her dressing gown when the door opened and the doctor stalked into the room.

'Sarah, I must talk to you.' He stood in front of her, his face serious. 'I didn't want to say anything in front of the others, but . . .'

'You can't talk to me here,' Sarah moved determinedly over to the door. She opened it and held it pointedly ajar. 'I'm at your service from nine in the morning until nine at night, but it's ten, and my time's my own, and I'm going to bed.'

He was very angry. He crossed the small room in two strides and caught her by the shoulders, pulling her clear of the door. Then, still holding her with one hand, he shut the door firmly with the other and propelled her back towards her bunk.

'You will listen to me.' He hissed the words between clenched teeth, and his grip was painfully tight. 'Sit down on that bunk and listen before I forget my own strength.'

Sarah flounced across the cabin and sat down on her bunk. Her heart was hammering. What on earth had she done now?

'Very well, I'm sitting down. I've obviously annoyed you, though I can't for the life of me think how.'

He walked across and sat down beside her. For a moment he stared at his hands, folded on his knees, then he passed a hand across his forehead in a gesture so weary that she almost repented of her indignant tone. Almost, but not quite. He had no right to burst into her cabin when she was in her nightie and demand that she listen to him!

'Where were you this afternoon between two and four o'clock?'

The question took her entirely by surprise. Her days were all busy but this one had been busier than most. She looked at him, a puzzled frown bringing her soft brows close.

'Gracious, I don't know! I helped Hughie wipe up after lunch, I took coffee to the bridge, yes I'm sure I did that . . .'

'I searched for you, Sarah. I wanted you to do some work for me. I looked in the sick bay, on deck, in the showers, I went into the galley, I . . .'

'What does it matter, anyway?' Sarah interrupted. 'It *was* my afternoon off, you said I could help Hughie because I'd worked late the evening before.' She nearly said that it was her own business what she did in her spare time, but something stopped her. 'Look, surely I can do what I like on my afternoon off?' She did not wish to mention that she had been doctoring the krill; his annoyance over that little episode was still too fresh for reminders.

'Only to an extent.' His eyes slid contemptuously from her face to the thin silk of the dressing gown covering her body. 'I checked everywhere for you. With one exception.' He paused, looking at her expectantly. 'Well? Aren't you going to ask me where I didn't look?'

'If it makes you happier, where didn't you look?'

'I didn't look in Wilde's cabin.' He was speaking through gritted teeth and the look on his face made Sarah quail. 'My *God*, when I think how you've lied to me, made a fool of me, made me believe you disliked the bloke, and now I find you've spent the best part of two hours . . .'

Sarah jumped to her feet. She was shaking all over, in the grip of a fury so righteous that for one moment she truly hated him.

'That's it. How dare you!' He stood up too, and she swung at his face with all her force. Her hand caught him across the cheek with a crack like a pistol shot, leaving five beautifully clear finger-prints etched upon the lean jaw. 'Get out of my cabin and stay out!'

She went to hurl open the cabin door, her temper roused to such an extent that the word caution was meaningless, and found herself grabbed and lifted right off her feet. He crushed her to his chest and carried her back across the cabin.

'Why, you little bitch!' He sat down on her bunk, still gripping her tightly in his arms. 'The sort of woman who sleeps with a man like Wilde doesn't slap my face and get away with it!

'I didn't sleep with him!' Sarah screamed, as he fairly hurled her onto the bunk. 'I was making the curry. I was behind the fridge when you came in be-cause we wanted it to be a secret, Hughie and me.'

His face was inches from hers. He loomed above her and she could see revenge in his eyes. She had no idea what he intended to do to her for slapping him but suddenly she was frightened, knowing that the tension which sizzled between them was not the sort of thing which could be easily put aside. She had been pushing against his chest as hard as she could but now she stopped and lay still as she saw her words sink in. She glanced down. One hand was on her shoulder, pinning her to the bed. The other held a handful of crumpled nylon nightdress. She knew, with appalling clarity, what he had meant to do and shivered, cold with fright. He could not believe her to be lying!

He saw her eyes go down to his hand and he let go

of the material. It was crushed from the fierceness of his grip. Slowly, he sat up, releasing her. He put a hand to his head.

'My God, I think you're driving me out of my mind—you and this confounded ship! Are you telling the truth this time or are you afraid of . . . ?'

'I am telling the truth.' Sarah spoke with all the sincerity at her command. 'I know this may seem strange to you, but I simply don't sleep around. I also know nurses sometimes get a reputation for doing just that, but you of all people should know that in nine out of ten cases it just isn't true. And I do think, sir, that you owe me an apology.'

He turned to look at her, running a hand through his dark hair. His expression was rueful and his mouth was actually opening to utter, she was sure, his very first apology, when there was a crunching, thundering roar, the ship lurched heavily, and all the lights went out.

'My God!'

'What on earth . . .'

They spoke simultaneously and must have moved simultaneously too, for the next thing she knew, Sarah was held tight in his arms and his mouth was seeking hers, moving hotly across her face whilst his hands slid up her back, turned her, and thrust her downwards so that she lay once more on the bunk with him on top of her.

'Are we sinking, Doctor?' She murmured the words against his lips, scarcely caring whether they were sinking or not, so sweet was his embrace. He did not attempt to answer her but his mouth covered hers, his tongue delicately probing her lips apart even as long, strong fingers found her breast, lifted it from its light nylon covering, touching the nipple to make it tighten in his grasp whilst his mouth continued to rouse her.

Her blood was racing and perhaps it was fear which brought her into the strong hair on the back of his head breathing hard, but when he lifted her without taking his mouth from hers she did not resist, not even when his mouth moved, roving across her throat, down to the little hollows of her collarbones, moving lower until, inexplicably, she felt his breath hot on her bare breasts. Where was her nightie, her silk dressing gown?

But the question did not need an answer, not whilst he held her like this, using her with such passion and tenderness. She moaned and arched her back when he moved away from her for a moment, begging him silently not to leave her, to continue with his lovemaking.

The light coming on again was like a bucket of cold water being flung over her. It brought her to her senses just about in time, she thought. They were both sprawled in utmost abandon across her bunk, and Dr Rothwell, blinking like an owl in the sudden brilliance, did not seem any too keen to stop his mad behaviour, either. Sarah sat up and dragged her nightie down round her knees. She was shaking, her body bruised from his weight. She felt a blush burn up across her body as he looked at her, sitting there all dishevelled. A hand went to her mouth. He would think her a real little tramp, just the sort of girl to sleep with Alan Wilde, to let a man who had come to her room in anger, for a talk, practically seduce her on her own bed. She began to weep and ducked her head forward so that her hair hid her tears, her hot and ashamed countenance.

'Sarah? Don't cry, my lovely.' He sounded anxious and concerned, not at all as if he despised her. 'It's all right, it was the sudden shock, that's all. I behaved badly, taking advantage of your fright, but I'm in command of myself again now, you've nothing to fear.' He had got up off the bed but now he returned to sit beside her and pull her into a comforting, brotherly embrace. She sagged gratefully against his chest, glad to hide her embarrassment and take comfort from his nearness.

'Will you be all right if I leave you, Sarah? I'd better check that there's nothing seriously wrong, though I don't think there is. I'll come back and let you know what happened.'

She nodded, though her whole newly awakened body screamed a negation. She would *not* be all right, ever again, without him! She longed to ask him to stay, to comfort her, yet there was a calm side of her mind which knew this would be a madness she would regret when he had taken inevitable advantage of her invitation, had loved her and left her, as he must.

'I'm sorry, Dr Rothwell. You must think I'm a s-slut, to let you . . . to behave the way I did. I don't understand it, I've never behaved like that in my life . . .'

He stood up, lifting her with him, and smoothed the dishevelled hair back from her brow. He let her lean against him but his arm round her was impersonal once more.

'It's all right, Sarah, we both behaved out of

character because fear makes us do strange things. Now you must . . .'

The door shot open. Stan stood there, white-faced. Behind him, Alan Wilde's startled features appeared.

'Are you all right, Sarah? We hit a growler, but it was . . .' Stan took in the scene. Sarah, leaning against the doctor's chest, her dressing gown lying on the floor, her face tearstained, her mouth smudged from his kisses. 'I say, what the devil . . .'

'It's all right, Stan. I came in to Sarah when the ship struck and we got thrown around a bit. What happened?'

The two men came right into the cabin. Alan looked at the bunk, with half the covers on the floor and the other half in great disarray. He glared at the doctor.

'Yes, Rothwell, what *did* happen? By the looks of it, a great deal!' He turned to Sarah. 'Are you all right, Sal? Was he . . . was he bothering you?'

Stan looked hunted.

'Shut up, Wilde.' He turned to the doctor. 'We struck a growler, Kurt, but as I said the captain sheered away so quickly that very little damage was done. Well, if you're both all right . . .'

'We are.' Dr Rothwell's voice was firm, cheery. 'In fact, I came visiting to ask Sarah if she'd marry me, and she said she would, so congratulations would be more in order than Alan's baleful glares.'

There was a stunned silence, then Alan spoke.

'Well, congratulations!' There was more than the hint of a sneer in the words. 'Not a moment too soon, by the look of this place!'

Sarah tensed, wondering whether to deny the

whole thing, but Kurt Rothwell was turning to the men, the hand round her shoulders tightening warningly.

'Ah, the engines are going full bore again. I'll come with you now and see what the Skipper has to say.' He turned to Sarah and, as she looked up at him, kissed her with tender possessiveness full on the mouth. 'Straight to bed now, doctor's orders! Goodnight, my love.'

The three men left the cabin, but Sarah just stood there. She felt as if she had been first run over by a steam roller and then hit with a heavy hammer. What on earth was happening? First Kurt Rothwell made vile accusations, then he made violent love, and then he pretended that they were engaged to be married, when barely forty-eight hours earlier he had told her there was someone ashore that he wanted to wed. Had the whole world gone mad, or was it just her? She stumbled over to her bunk and tumbled in, dragging the covers up over her head. What a mess it all was, and if the doctor thought that telling lies would make it easier he was very much mistaken. What would happen when they got ashore? They could pretend to argue, she supposed, and break off the fictitious engagement before they docked. But, so far as she could see, he had created a difficult situation for everyone. Before, people had talked about her and Alan. Now, they would talk about her and Kurt Rothwell.

Sarah turned her head into the pillow, then realised that the light was still on. Damn, damn and damn again, she would have to get out of bed and switch it off. She got out of bed and as she crossed the cabin, glanced at herself in the mirror. She looked extremely sexy in the flimsy nightie with her hair tumbling carelessly across her bare shoulders. Could any of it have been her fault? But she had not invited Kurt Rothwell in to her cabin, far less to tear her clothes off and make love to her on her bunk.

She turned off the light and padded back to bed, cuddling down quickly. No way, she decided, could she be blamed for the false position that she now found herself in. She had been shamefully treated by the doctor, and if he suffered as a result of the spoof engagement, then it was a just punishment for some very unpleasant behaviour. Yes, it was all his fault, he was selfish, domineering and incredibly conceited. He was a beast, in fact, and she was very unlucky ever to have landed a job with him. The sooner they got ashore and could part company for ever, the better pleased she ought to be.

She sighed, and rubbed her arms. How she ached! It was cold and lonely in this bed. Her mind went wistfully back to the moment when he had held her, then she jerked her thoughts severely back into a more conventional line. Stan had come in and put a stop to Dr Rothwell's dreadful, uninhibited goings-on, and a good thing too!

Strong-mindedly, she told herself to go to sleep and forget him. And she obeyed at least one of these injunctions before many moments had passed.

CHAPTER TEN

IT WAS not easy to act naturally next morning, when
they met in the sickbay to do the clinic, but Sarah
was determined to do her best. She had breakfasted
with the men and had suffered the doubtful pleasure of being congratulated on her engagement—
news of any sort travelled fast. One glance at Dr
Rothwell's face, as he entered the sick bay, made
her sure that he had been performing the same
task, but she smiled at him, determined to retain at
least the pretence of a friendly atmosphere.

'Good morning, Doctor. I wondered if I might
have a few words with you, before the first patients
arrive?'

'Certainly, Nurse.'

'It's about last night. Doctor, I realise you were
motivated by kindness, but I've decided I'd really
much rather not enter into the sort of pretence
which is called for, if you don't mind. It's quite
simple, really, we'll just put it around that we've
quarrelled. After all, nothing happened which
shouldn't have, last night, it was only that appear-
ances were a bit against us.'

He gave her a sardonic glance, his eyebrows
rising.

'I was motivated by kindness, was I? Well, in that
case, I'm motivated by it still. No, Nurse Barford, I
will not release you from our engagement so that
you can continue to flirt with other team members.

Besides, being engaged to you will bring with it certain . . . privileges, which I don't intend to forego.'

Sarah stiffened. He really could be outrageous.

'But Doctor, you told me you were contemplating marriage when we reach home. It will be difficult to explain to the team that you don't want to have your engagement talked about, surely? Your—your lady-friend will be hurt, at the very least.'

'That's my affair, Nurse. And now . . . come here, please.'

He was holding the treatment book. Sarah went over to him and peered at the page he appeared to be studying.

'Yes, sir? Have I done something wrong?'

She looked enquiringly up at him, and was seized and soundly kissed despite her indignant struggles. Breaking free she glared up at him, her chest heaving, her heart pattering.

'Really, Dr Rothwell, this is becoming monotonous. If that's one of your "privileges", then you'll just have to forego it.'

'Don't pretend that you hate my kisses, because it isn't true.' His voice was heavy with sarcasm. 'You like being kissed. And cuddled. In fact, you thoroughly enjoy lovemaking, and why not, so don't tighten your lips at me, Nurse!'

'I do *not*! Oh, I know I got carried away last night, but I was about to come to my senses when the lights came on. As for enjoying your lovemaking, that is the most conceited, self-satisfied remark I ever heard!'

'What a little liar you are,' Dr Rothwell said

affably, moving over to the door. 'But if you don't enjoy it, then I must say, being repulsed by you is a very pleasant experience. Do you always clutch a man you hate, Nurse?'

'Dr Rothwell, I . . .'

He opened the door and the first patient entered, effectively forcing Sarah to break off her tirade before it had even begun. She hastily turned her back and hurried to the side cupboard where most of her equipment for doing obs. was kept. She knew that her face must be red, and that everyone would assume she and the doctor . . .

Damn him, she said to herself. She could not tell him that his lovemaking disturbed her deeply, because there could be no future in letting him possess her. She did not believe in casual affairs, did not wish to indulge in them, and not only did Dr Rothwell have a girl he intended to marry ashore, but there were times when he did not even seem to like her, let alone love her. She turned round at last, and saw that no one was staring at her, that the crew member being treated was laughing over something the doctor had said, scarcely sparing her a glance. Perhaps, after all, this stupid false engagement nonsense would not affect her too much.

'Good morning, my love.'

Sarah, who was finding the fictional engagement more and more infuriating, tried to elude the doctor as they crossed the mess deck, he on his way from breakfast, she on her way to it. But her attempt was foiled and she was neatly captured, kissed, and replaced, so to speak, on her breakfast-path. Blushing furiously, she went and sat down beside Stan, who grinned at her.

'Why so shy, Sarah? It's only natural that your fiancé should want to give you a kiss. Is it because we all watch with such envy?'

'Not really. It's because I feel he's marking ownership, so to speak.'

Stan reached across the table for another piece of toast, then spoke thickly through a mouthful.

'I know what you mean, of course, but you must have realised by now that the Doc's quite possessive. Alan was saying that Kurt all but growled when you slipped on deck yesterday, and Alan picked you up.'

Sarah giggled at the remembered incident.

'Yes, that's true, he did. Frankly, if I'd known about his possessiveness I'd never have agreed to the engagement in the first place. I feel he's watching me, whatever I'm doing and wherever I go. It's disconcerting.'

'Then tell him, girl.' Stan crunched toast. 'I've never thought of Kurt as a jealous bloke, and I'm sure if you told him to move back a bit, he would. He's deeply in love with you, any fool can see that.'

Deeply in love, Sarah scoffed silently. Deeply concerned with making sure that I don't step out of line with one of his beloved team! But out loud she merely said, 'I'll think about it, Stan.'

'You do that.' He got up, looking down at her. 'You're a bit in awe of him still, aren't you, despite the engagement? You hardly ever call him by his first name, and you colour and jump when he calls you over for something. Would you like me to have a word with him for you? He wouldn't resent it, coming from me. We've been pals too long.'

'No thanks, Stan, but thanks all the same.' Sarah sipped her coffee and watched Stan's back view disappearing through the mess deck door. He was a nice chap, totally different from his pal.

Sarah glanced at her fob watch. Good, she had ten minutes before the clinic started. She would have egg and bacon, if Hughie had any left. She went to the hatch, collected a plate laden with bacon, eggs, fried bread and tomatoes, and took it back to the table. Beginning to eat, she reflected on the past couple of days. In truth, things could have been a lot worse. In public, Dr Rothwell was every inch a fiancé, kissing her when he could find an excuse for so doing, standing with his hand on her waist or shoulder, calling her pet-names. That, of course, was outside clinic hours. When they were working, she was a nurse and he was a doctor, and that suited her very well.

What really surprised her, though, was his attitude to her in private. She had expected to have to fight him off, thinking that he would use the fictitious engagement to try to make love to her, but apart from the one kiss in the sickbay on the very first morning, there had been nothing. Not a word, not a glance was out of place with the doctor-nurse relationship which existed in the sickbay. He could have been talking to his old mother, Sarah thought resentfully, for all the interest he put in to their discussions.

Of course, she was glad he took this attitude, she told herself primly. Very glad. But she could not help wondering what was so repulsive about her that he no longer sought her out in her cabin or anywhere else, that even when circumstances forced them to be alone together he never so much as squeezed her hand. I've given him opportunities enough, she told herself now, and not one of them has he taken advantage of. Slipping on the deck, she had cut her knees. Who put on the dressing, when they had been cleaned? She had done it herself, since Dr Rothwell seemed to feel she could manage. She had asked him to undo her string of pearls the previous evening, when they had got entangled with the thick curls at the nape of her neck. He had done it without once letting his fingers rest on her skin, though she was tingling with anticipation all the while he was in her room. Of course, I'm glad he's being so sensible, she told herself glumly. It just seems strange, that's all.

Getting to her feet with her now empty plate, Sarah carried it over to the hatch. As she crossed the room, she noticed, or thought she noticed, a slight difference in the way the ship was riding the waves. She poked her head through the hatch and hailed the cook.

'Hey, Hughie, here's some more washing up. Is it still cold and dark out on deck?'

Hughie turned from the sink.

'Aye, though not dark for so long. You saw daylight yesterday, didn't you? For half an hour or more, I heard. Why do you ask?'

'Well, the ship feels different. Heavy, slower, something like that. I wondered if being in calmer seas had that effect?'

'We'll make a seaman of you yet!' Hughie beamed approvingly. 'No, the chief's been having trouble with one of the engines, nothing to worry about, but it's cut down our speed. But it won't stop us making harbour in four days, he says.'

Sarah's heart gave an uncharacteristic lurch. She chided herself. She was *glad* they only had another four days aboard the *Ice Venture*, *glad* they would soon dock so that she and Kurt Rothwell could go their separate ways. And she would get a cruise ship, she was almost sure of it, and flirt with heavenly, handsome sailors and rich passengers, and bask in the sun, and wear beautiful clothes. And miss Dr Rothwell hellishly.

The last thought made her blink. Absurd, to miss someone who had made this voyage such a difficult business. She left the mess deck and trudged down the corridor to the sickbay. She was suffering from being cribbed, cabinned and confined, that was the trouble! Stuck in this tiny ship with the same people for weeks on end, she had allowed herself to think that it was the whole world and that Kurt Rothwell was the only person who mattered to her. Once she got ashore, into the fresh air, she would speedily see that there were other, and much nicer, fish in the sea. She giggled at her own simile—could she think of nothing but sea and ships?

She entered the sickbay. Dr Rothwell was sitting at the desk, filling page after page with his tiny, indecipherable scrawl. Sarah sighed and squared her shoulders. Another day was about to start.

Sarah was in her bunk and fast asleep when the engines stopped. She woke in that split second, knowing that something was different, that something was missing, without knowing what. She lay there, listening.

Then all hell was let loose. The ship lurched into a trough with the familiar movement which Sarah knew so well, and then began to climb out. But she was powerless, rudderless, for a sufficient length of time for a wave, larger and stronger than the rest, to have her at its mercy. It seized the ship and tipped her violently forward, then spun her round and smashed against her side.

Sarah was shot out of her bunk and across the cabin in the pitch dark, to strike her head and shoulder painfully against the opposite bulkhead. Before she could do more than gasp and fling out a hand the ship tilted in the opposite direction every bit as violently and she was hurled back against her bunk. Then the ship seemed to stand on her head, and it seemed that Sarah was also standing on hers; for the next few moments indeed, her feet were the only part of her anatomy she did not stand on. She was hurled around her small cabin like a dice being rattled in a cup. She was struck by or struck against every article in the place, at one moment she found herself clutching at what should have been the floor, only to find it was her locker. Dizzy and sick, she clung there until the locker seemed to decide it had had enough of her and flung her off, to careen across the polished floorboards and end up clutching with desperate strength at her sturdy bunk.

Then, sweetest of sounds, she heard the engines cough, clatter, and buzz into life once more. The ship steadied, and Sarah staggered to her feet, crossed the cabin, and pressed the light switch. A glance round confirmed that the place would never be quite the same again, but that was not worrying her.

Kurt! Was he all right, was he alive, even? The fact that there were seventeen other men who might equally well be dead or injured scarcely occurred to her. She must get to Kurt, make sure that he was not lying desperately injured in some part of the ship.

She snatched a thick sweater off the floor and dragged it on, then set off down the corridor. She banged on his cabin door then flung it open.

'Kurt?' He was half under his bunk, lying on his stomach. Her heart skipped a beat. Was he unconscious, was his head horribly crushed against the opposite bulkhead? She dropped to her knees, flinging her arms round him, towing him out with the utmost care whilst she babbled on.

'My poor darling, are you much hurt? The engines stopped, and all I could think of was . . .'

She stopped short. He was very much alive and grinning broadly at her over his shoulder. He was also getting to his feet, obviously as physically fit as she.

'I'm fine, thank you, my love, I was just fishing out my shoes. They slid under the bunk, and . . .' his eyes took in her dishevelled appearance, the sweater over the flimsy nightie. 'What's happened to you, then?'

He was adept at bringing down the emotional temperature, Sarah thought ruefully, scrambling to her feet. What had she said? In the heat of the moment had she given herself away?

'I got thrown out of bed and hurled round my cabin a bit.' She eyed him resentfully. Why had he not been taken by surprise? She voiced the thought aloud. 'I take it that you really are all right, that you didn't even suffer bruising?'

'That's right. I was reading, and heard the engines go off. I clung, of course, but it was only for a few seconds. Then the Chief got the engines going again and we came back to normal.' He led her to the door, a casual hand at her waist. 'Go back and dress, there's a good girl, and come straight to the sickbay. I daresay we'll have work to do—the fellows in the engine room may have suffered a bit.'

She was halfway down the corridor when he called after her. She turned, brows raised.

'Yes, sir?'

'One day soon I'll remind you of tonight!'

She whisked round and continued down the corridor. Oh, damn it, he had heard whatever foolish things she had muttered when she feared he had been badly injured. But there was no time to think about it. Limping down the corridor towards her were two members of the crew, one of them bleeding from a deep gash over his eye. She and Dr Rothwell were both going to be very busy for a while.

'One Zimmer splint, sir, and that's the last.' Sarah yawned widely before she could prevent herself. 'Sorry, but I'm worn out, we seem to have been patching up for hours.'

Dr Rothwell looked pale too, his eyes dark, but he came over to her patient.

'Just a broken finger? Look, I'll take over now, Sarah. You clear away. And then I think we deserve some rest.'

'You both deserve a medal, I think,' Albert said as Sarah walked wearily over to the trolley. 'Just the two of you toiling away amongst broken bones and gore—just what happened on the bridge, anyway?'

'A pane of glass shattered, which was why three of the crew were badly cut.' Dr Rothwell smiled at Sarah. 'Any inexperience with suturing has been made good tonight, eh, Nurse?'

'Mm hmm, I could stitch in my sleep,' Sarah admitted. 'What about the mess, sir? The floor's filthy.'

She expected him to tell her to leave it, but he did not.

'There you are, Albert!' The doctor patted the last patient on the shoulder. 'Now I've finished with Albert's broken finger, I'll give you a hand to clear up. Is there a mop handy?'

'Yes. I'll get it.'

The two of them, too tired for talk, worked silently side by side until the floor shone and all the surfaces were clean and tidy once more. Then Kurt Rothwell heaved a deep sigh.

'I could sleep for a week and I daresay you feel the same, but it's clinic as usual in the morning, Sarah. Never mind, we'll be docking in three days and then we'll be able to have a real rest. Shall I give you a call around eight?'

'I suppose someone had better, or I probably would sleep for a week.' Sarah headed for the door. 'Goodnight, Doctor. Or should it be good morning?'

'It should be good morning, but we'll settle for goodnight!'

He made his way to his cabin without a backward glance, but Sarah was too worn out to feel resentful at his lack of interest. All she wanted was to sleep, and sleep she would, the moment her head touched the pillow. She entered her cabin and flung herself down on the bunk, half-waking to a recollection that she was fully dressed, then falling asleep again before a possible solution, like undressing, had occurred to her.

Sarah was packing when the knock came on her cabin door. She called out 'Come in,' and then turned back to her task, knowing that Hughie had promised to send her a snack and a cup of coffee along at mid-morning and thinking that it was he.

It was indeed the coffee, but Dr Rothwell was carrying it, and some sandwiches wrapped in greaseproof paper. He smiled at her across the small room, then handed her one cup of coffee and took the other over to her bunk. Sitting down, he patted the covers beside him.

'Come and relax for a few minutes. We've worked hard enough, in all conscience, these past three days.'

Sarah sat down beside him and sipped at her hot coffee, then stood it down on the small bedside table and bit into a sandwich.

'That's true. I'm going to take your advice once we get ashore and sleep for a week.'

'Oh, yes? You aren't going to paint the town red with Alan and Albert and the lads?'

'Scarcely! I'm engaged to you, if you remember, or at least everyone on board this ship thinks I am. No, I think I'll go home, have that rest we were talking about, and then perhaps try to get taken on by a cruise ship.' She glanced across at him. He was eyeing her quizzically, the hint of a smile on his mouth. 'Well? You did say you'd give me a good reference.'

'If you wanted one, I said.'

'I want one,' Sarah said promptly. 'After these past weeks, I feel like some sunshine and carefree living. The shopping will be fun, too. I've not seen a shop or another woman for all these weeks, so I may well go berserk and buy all sorts of unsuitable things.'

'You might. Why not get a wedding dress?'

Sarah shot him a quick, startled look. What exactly did he mean by that?

'Why should I? I'm not thinking of getting married.'

He put his arm round her shoulders, turning her so that she was facing him.

'Aren't you? Are you quite sure about that? Most engagements end in marriage, after all.'

'Oh yes, but not engagements like ours.' Her face was hot with embarrassment, for she saw it all, now. Stupidly telling him that she would not be painting the town red with the boys had made him feel a little guilty, made him feel that he had spoiled her chances with Alan, as indeed he had. Except that the last thing she wanted was an involvement with any of the men aboard. Except one, and he was going to get married to some girl he had met. 'Besides, you know very well that you're getting married as soon as we get ashore.'

'So I am. Why don't you come to the wedding? Before rushing off to Norfolk to sleep for a week, of course!'

Sitting there, with the warm weight of his arm

about her shoulders, Sarah suddenly saw the whole scene. Kurt, dark-suited, serious, with the expression on his face which she most loved to see. He was looking down at a ravishing brunette, clad all in bridal white, with a half-smile on his lips, and she, Sarah, was standing nearby watching them both, whilst her world turned to ashes. She admitted to herself, for the first time, that she loved Kurt Rothwell with all her heart and wanted nothing more out of life than to be with him. But it was no use wishing. The die was cast, the ship within a few hours of the shores of England, and she must salvage her pride, continue to pretend indifference.

'Oh, no, I couldn't possibly come to your wedding, Dr Rothwell, though it's very nice of you to ask me. You once wanted to know if there was a man, at home, and I probably gave you to understand that there was no one. But this voyage has made me realise that I lied to you, quite unwittingly. I'm not in love with Jack Winters, but I do believe I love . . . well, someone else. So you see I can't wait to get home.'

She sounded just right, bright, a little wistful, completely honest. She glanced timidly at his face. Would it do? Had he been fooled? His face looked strange, white and still, with a stiffness about the mouth and a tautness over his cheekbones. Then he shrugged and stood up.

'I won't over-persuade you, Sarah, I know how embarrassing that can be.' He held out his hand. 'I'll say goodbye now, because we may be too busy for farewells, later. If there's . . .'

Even as she got to her feet, a fearful sound rent

the air. Louder than a bull, shriller than a siren, it boomed and re-echoed round the small cabin.

It was too much for Sarah. She took a flying leap forward, and landed in Dr Rothwell's arms just as the sound boomed out again.

And his arms went round her, tightly, holding her close. His mouth came down on hers, in a deep, passionate kiss which left her breathless. And then, whilst she still clung, heart hammering, he calmly lifted her off her feet and carried her over to the bunk. He sat down with her on his knee. He was grinning broadly, but there was a glitter in his eye which had nothing to do with mirth.

'Sarah, sweet Sarah, I love you! Now tell me you love me.' His mouth took hers again, gagging her, then moved leisurely across her throat whilst his hands slid up beneath her sweater, touching her tingling flesh, tugging her satin bra aside so that he could fondle her breasts. 'How you've lied to me, my darling, and how I'll make you regret it!'

'No! Stop it, I haven't, I didn't . . .' Sarah registered his words, wide-eyed. 'Kurt, did you say you *loved* me?'

'More than I ever thought I could love anyone. And you, Nurse Barford, had better either admit that you love me too, or explain why you suddenly landed in my arms just now.'

'I—I—I . . .' stammered Sarah, her face inches from his. 'I was frightened by that awful noise, that was why I jumped at you. Do stop it, do let me go! You know very well you're only being nice to me because you stopped me seeing Alan or any of the others.' She sniffed. 'Not that I cared for that. And you're getting married.' She sat up straighter and pushed hard against his chest, his imprisoning arms. 'Let me go, you don't mean a word of it.'

She jerked convulsively in his grip, trying to free herself but he gave her a hard, white grin and held on.

'Oh no you don't, Sarah, no more running, and no more misunderstandings, either. It's *you* I intend to marry, you little dope, and I've told you I love you. Now lie if you dare.'

'You want to marry *me*? Well, all I can say is your behaviour hasn't been exactly loverlike!' She sighed as he kissed down the side of her face, then took her mouth, his touch tender. She freed herself for an instant. 'Oh, Kurt, I love you so much.'

After that there was silence for a little. Then Sarah called a halt to behaviour which was certainly loverlike, if not very dignified.

'Kurt, if you wanted to marry me, why were you so horrid? I mean there we were, engaged, and you never so much as squeezed my hand—except to annoy the others, of course.'

Kurt sighed and stroked her shining, tumbled curls.

'Because I wanted to give you a fair chance, that's why. After all, courtship on board a distant water trawler is, of necessity, somewhat limited. I couldn't take you out for a meal, or on deck to admire the moonlight, or for a drive. I couldn't even suggest a quiet evening by the fireside. To be blunt, love, there was only one way I could show you how I felt, and . . . well, half-measures never have satisfied me. I knew if I started anything I'd want to finish it, and I soon realised that you were the same. No, don't hit me, it's unladylike!'

'I don't mind you admitting that you're sex-mad, but you shouldn't pretend that I am as well,' Sarah grumbled. 'You shocked me into letting you make love to me, that's what you did. Otherwise I should have kept you at arm's length.'

'I see. Like you are now?' Kurt's voice was bland but the gleam in his eyes was not. 'Anyway, it was the behaviour of the *Ice Venture* which shocked you, not my carryings-on.'

'I was equally shocked by you both,' Sarah said firmly, cuddling up. 'Oh Kurt, I love you so. If only we could be married as soon as . . . Oh, oh, oh!'

The fearful noise which had precipitated her into his arms once already, boomed round the cabin again. Kurt tumbled her onto the bunk, then lay down beside her.

'That's better! I can get at you now.'

'No, not for a minute,' Sarah begged. She was trembling, and not entirely from fright. 'Kurt, what *is* that noise?'

He pulled her close, then spoke against the soft skin of her neck.

'The foghorn of course. It's nasty, out there.' He smiled at her. 'I shall have to buy one for our honeymoon—it has certainly achieved some startling results today!'

'A foghorn?' Sarah relaxed, pressing closer. 'There you are again, you see. I was tricked into landing in your arms earlier, I thought we were sinking.'

'Well, tricked or not, that's where you've ended up. In fact, since we're approaching the East Coast right now, in thick fog, that foghorn's going to keep on booming. So I'm going to keep a good, firm hold on you. God knows where you'll jump next time, unless I do. Right?'

'Kurt, you're awful! But I love you.'

Moments later the foghorn sounded again, then again, as the *Ice Venture* made her way cautiously into the estuary. On the bridge, the captain and his mate kept their eyes fixed on the radar and the swirling whiteness of the fog. They had slowed right down, but they knew the reaches of the estuary and the locks like the palms of their hands. They would dock as they had planned. The foghorn boomed warningly, again and again.

Below, Sarah lay in Kurt's arms, and never heard a sound!

Doctor Nurse Romances

Amongst the intense emotional pressures of modern medical life, doctors and nurses often find romance. Read about their lives and loves in the other three Doctor Nurse titles available this month.

TREAD SOFTLY, NURSE
by Lynne Collins

'Avoid throwing yourself at a man – it's always a mistake.'
Why should the arrogant Mr Duffy care if Nurse Tiffany Kane ruins her reputation and loses her job because of a silly infatuation? For she loathes *him* with a startling intensity.

DR VENABLES' PRACTICE
by Anne Vinton

The position of Nurse-Receptionist in Dr Laurence Venables' Harley Street practice is viewed with mixed feelings by Staff Nurse Penny Hunt. For, despite his extreme good looks, the distinguished Dr Venables makes her hackles rise – even when he isn't trying!

SHAMROCK NURSE
by Elspeth O'Brien

Nurse Nuala Kavanagh, sent to nurse Blake Wendover after the surgeon's eyes have been accidentally damaged, is as concerned as the rest of St.Jude's staff about his sight. Will she ever be more than a softly-voiced, gentle presence to him?

Mills & Boon
the rose of romance